Blessing

Omega Queen Series, Volume 8

W.J. May

Published by Dark Shadow Publishing, 2021.

This is a work of fiction. Similarities to real people, places, or events are entirely coincidental.

BLESSING

First edition. January 20, 2021.

Copyright © 2021 W.J. May.

Written by W.J. May.

Also by W.J. May

Bit-Lit Series
Lost Vampire
Cost of Blood
Price of Death

Blood Red Series
Courage Runs Red
The Night Watch
Marked by Courage
Forever Night
The Other Side of Fear
Blood Red Box Set Books #1-5

Daughters of Darkness: Victoria's Journey
Victoria
Huntress
Coveted (A Vampire & Paranormal Romance)
Twisted
Daughter of Darkness - Victoria - Box Set

Great Temptation Series
The Devil's Footsteps
Heaven's Command
Mortals Surrender

Hidden Secrets Saga
Seventh Mark - Part 1
Seventh Mark - Part 2
Marked By Destiny
Compelled
Fate's Intervention
Chosen Three
The Hidden Secrets Saga: The Complete Series

Kerrigan Chronicles
Stopping Time
A Passage of Time
Ticking Clock
Secrets in Time
Time in the City
Ultimate Future
Guilt Of My Past

Mending Magic Series
Lost Souls
Illusion of Power

Challenging the Dark
Castle of Power
Limits of Magic
Protectors of Light

Omega Queen Series
Discipline
Bravery
Courage
Conquer
Strength
Validation
Approval
Blessing

Paranormal Huntress Series
Never Look Back
Coven Master
Alpha's Permission
Blood Bonding
Oracle of Nightmares
Shadows in the Night
Paranormal Huntress BOX SET

Prophecy Series
Only the Beginning
White Winter
Secrets of Destiny

Revamped Series
Hidden
Banished
Converted

Royal Factions
The Price For Peace
The Cost for Surviving
The Punishment For Deception
Faking Perfection
The Most Cherished
The Strength to Endure

The Chronicles of Kerrigan
Rae of Hope
Dark Nebula
House of Cards
Royal Tea
Under Fire
End in Sight
Hidden Darkness
Twisted Together
Mark of Fate
Strength & Power
Last One Standing
Rae of Light
The Chronicles of Kerrigan Box Set Books # 1 - 6

The Chronicles of Kerrigan: Gabriel
Living in the Past
Present For Today
Staring at the Future

The Chronicles of Kerrigan Prequel
Christmas Before the Magic
Question the Darkness
Into the Darkness
Fight the Darkness
Alone in the Darkness
Lost in Darkness
The Chronicles of Kerrigan Prequel Series Books #1-3

The Chronicles of Kerrigan Sequel
A Matter of Time
Time Piece
Second Chance
Glitch in Time
Our Time
Precious Time

The Hidden Secrets Saga
Seventh Mark (part 1 & 2)

The Kerrigan Kids
School of Potential
Myths & Magic
Kith & Kin
Playing With Power
Line of Ancestry
Descent of Hope
Illusion of Shadows
Frozen by the Future

The Queen's Alpha Series
Eternal
Everlasting
Unceasing
Evermore
Forever
Boundless
Prophecy
Protected
Foretelling
Revelation
Betrayal
Resolved
The Queen's Alpha Box Set

The Senseless Series
Radium Halos - Part 1
Radium Halos - Part 2

Nonsense
Perception
The Senseless - Box Set Books #1-4

Standalone
Shadow of Doubt (Part 1 & 2)
Five Shades of Fantasy
Zwarte Nevel
Shadow of Doubt - Part 1
Shadow of Doubt - Part 2
Four and a Half Shades of Fantasy
Dream Fighter
What Creeps in the Night
Forest of the Forbidden
Arcane Forest: A Fantasy Anthology
The First Fantasy Box Set

Watch for more at www.wjmaybooks.com.

Copyright 2021 by W.J. May

THIS E-BOOK OR PRINT is licensed for your personal enjoyment only. This e-book/paperback may not be re-sold or given away to other people. If you would like to share this book with another person, please purchase an additional copy for each recipient. If you're reading this book and did not purchase it, or it was not purchased for your use only, then please return to Smashwords.com and purchase your own copy. Thank you for respecting the hard work of the author.

All rights reserved. No part of this publication may be reproduced, stored in or introduced into a retrieval system, or transmitted, in any form, or by any means (electronic, mechanical, photocopying, recording, or otherwise) without the prior written permission of both the copyright owner and the above publisher of this book.

This is a work of fiction. Names, characters, places, brands, media, and incidents are either the product of the author's imagination or are used fictitiously. Any resemblance to actual person, living or dead, events, or locales is entirely coincidental. The author acknowledges the trademarked status and trademark owners of various products referenced in this work of fiction, which have been used without permission. The publication/use of these trademarks is not authorized, associated with, or sponsored by the trademark owners.

All rights reserved.
Copyright 2021 by W.J. May
Blessing, Book 8 of the Omega Queen Series
Cover design by: Book Cover by Design

No part of this book may be used or reproduced in any manner whatsoever without written permission, except in the case of brief quotations embodied in articles and reviews.

Have You Read the C.o.K Series?

The Chronicles of Kerrigan
Book I - *Rae of Hope* is FREE!

BOOK TRAILER:
http://www.youtube.com/watch?v=gILAwXxx8MU

How hard do you have to shake the family tree to find the truth about the past?

Fifteen year-old Rae Kerrigan never really knew her family's history. Her mother and father died when she was young and it is only when she accepts a scholarship to the prestigious Guilder Boarding School in England that a mysterious family secret is revealed.

Will the sins of the father be the sins of the daughter?

As Rae struggles with new friends, a new school and a star-struck forbidden love, she must also face the ultimate challenge: receive a tattoo on her sixteenth birthday with specific powers that may bind her to an unspeakable darkness. It's up to Rae to undo the dark evil in her family's past and have a ray of hope for her future.

Find W.J. May

Website:
https://www.wjmaybooks.com
Facebook:
https://www.facebook.com/pages/Author-WJ-May-FAN-PAGE/141170442608149
Newsletter:
SIGN UP FOR W.J. May's Newsletter to find out about new releases, updates, cover reveals and even freebies!
http://eepurl.com/97aYf

Blessing Blurb:

USA Today Bestselling author, W.J. May, continues the highly anticipated bestselling YA/NA series about love, betrayal, magic and fantasy.

Be prepared to fight... it's the only option.

What do you say when the dead come knocking...?

When an unexpected visitor shows up from the past, Evie's world flips upside-down. A long kept secret is forced into the open, as the enemy they've been racing is finally given a name.

Time is running out. But this quest isn't something they can do on their own.

Can they unite what's left of the five kingdoms? Can they fulfill the prophecy and find the missing stone in time? Or has their adventure been doomed to fail from the start?

Only time will tell...

BE CAREFUL WHO YOU trust. Even the devil was once an angel.

The Queen's Alpha Series

Eternal
Everlasting
Unceasing
Evermore
Forever
Boundless
Prophecy
Protected
Foretelling
Revelation
Betrayal
Resolved

The Omega Queen Series

Discipline
Bravery
Courage
Conquer
Strength
Validation
Approval
Blessing
Balance
Grievance
Enchanted
Gratified

Chapter 1

Evie woke up in a bed she didn't know, in a place she didn't recognize, under the watchful eyes of a dozen people she'd seen a million times before.

She stared without blinking. The paintings stared back.

The early evening sun peeked through the curtains and it came back to her like something out of a dream. She'd gone for a walk in the forest. She'd run into some trouble. There may have been some fire involved. She may have fallen over the side of a cliff.

She hadn't been alone.

"Ellanden."

Her voice croaked out and she sat up quickly, only to fall right back down on the bed. There was something the matter with her head. Like someone had weighted it with invisible stones.

Where am I?

She looked around more slowly, being incredibly ginger with her neck. It was a house of some kind—but a house unlike any she'd ever seen. It seemed to go up more than out. The room on the ground floor was incredibly small—with little else than a grill for cooking and a simple table and chairs—but there was a wooden stairwell in the middle that stretched right into the clouds.

"...Ellanden?" she called again, barely a whisper.

There was movement in the corner, a subtle shifting by the wall. She strained upwards to see a huddled form under a pile of blankets. It rose and fell slowly; he must have been asleep.

If that's even him!

She threw herself to the floor in a sudden panic as more bits of memory started to leak through. There had been slavers. A pair of them. They'd knocked her off the mountain and taken Ellanden hostage. She'd been too disoriented to see what exactly they'd done to him.

But there had been blood. Lots of blood.

Please be him...please be him...

She dragged herself along the floor in the most undignified way possible, wondering every few seconds what in the world must have happened to her head. A few times she reached up a hand to touch it, but she was disturbed by the texture she found there and decided it was better left alone.

When at last she reached the far corner, she was flushed and out of breath. With a clumsy hand she reached up and yanked off the blankets, only to find a set of piercing immortal eyes.

"That was the most pathetic thing I've ever seen."

She collapsed against the bed in a mixture of relief and exhaustion, swinging a blind hand to smack him at the same time. Whatever had happened, wherever they were—he was alive and talking.

They could take it from there.

"Are you all right?" she whispered when she could finally pull in a breath. "Do you remember anything that happened?"

The fae sat up slowly, shaking his head.

Despite that signature charm, he was clearly in a bad state. Fresh bandages had been wrapped around his chest with obvious care, but his hands were bloody and there were leaves in his hair.

"No, not really."

His voice was rough, too. And quiet enough to scare her.

"I remember a fire..." he began slowly. "...a blinding fire. And there was..." He paused suddenly, lifting a bracing hand to his chest. "You saved me...by throwing me off a mountain."

Not clear whether that was a good or a bad thing.

Evie beamed smugly, thinking it rather obvious.

"That sounds like me," she panted, hoisting herself higher. "Typical hero stuff—and you, the helpless damsel." Ignoring his painful grimace she crawled onto the bed, finding her balance before lifting a hand to her temple. "Tell me honestly, is there something wrong with my head?"

"Yes," he answered automatically.

"No—*look* at it. Seriously. I think there's something wrong."

His eyes flitted up before widening in sudden surprise. For a moment, it looked like he was trying to figure it out himself. Then his face cleared with a sudden smile.

"You look fine. It's a vast improvement."

Her cheeks paled with sudden dread. "What does that—"

A noise sounded in the distance and they abruptly fell quiet.

There was nothing overtly threatening about the little house. Quite the contrary, in spite of its strange design, the place was downright cozy. It made them feel protected. Drowsy. Safe.

Just like the witch's cabin. Just like the wizard's cave.

"Evie, I don't think I can stand," Ellanden breathed, keeping his eyes on the window. A sun-swept lawn stretched just outside, bordered by wildflowers and a tiny wooden fence. "Do you have a weapon? Could you manage some fire?"

She shook her head faintly, following his gaze.

There were footsteps, still a good way off but getting steadily closer. If it wasn't for her father's shifter blood, she probably wouldn't have been able to hear them. And while they might have been kept alive, even perhaps dragged out of harm's way, the only thing her mind could register was that they'd been brought there against their will. And the house only had one door.

"We'll have to make a run for it," she said, heaving herself up at the same time. As soon as she did the room tilted, and she fell back onto the fae's chest. "Okay...maybe we'll walk."

There was a muffled gasp, and a strong hand flung her to the floor.

"Seven hells—Everly!"

The fae leaned back painfully, feeling the bandages on his chest. A bloom of blood had seeped through the second it made contact with her elbow and the world was suddenly unsteady.

Her mouth fell open in shock.

"Holy crap—Ellanden! You're still bleeding!"

His eyes found her slowly before closing in a silent prayer.

"Not today," he told himself quietly. "But soon. When she thinks she's safe. When she's not expecting..."

"What are you saying?"

"Nothing." He lifted himself higher, paling with the effort. Twice he tried swinging his legs off the bed, but he stopped short both times. "I'm not sure walking away is in the cards. But if *you* can get out—go right now. Try to shift and get back to the fort. Before whoever's coming—"

But however he was going to finish that sentence, they'd never know. Because at that exact moment, the door flew open and a beautiful woman stepped into the house.

For a split second, both teenagers just stared—frozen with identical looks of shock.

Then Evie lifted a hand to her head.

"Seven hells..." she murmured faintly. "It's worse than I thought..."

WHEN EVIE WAS A LITTLE girl she used to wander the halls of her mother's castle, looking up at the royal portraits. Dreaming about what it would be like if those people were to step out of their ancient frames and walk the halls beside her—gifted with a sudden burst of life.

Each one came with their own legend. Each one came with their own story.

But she'd always liked one story the best.

Her grandmother, Adelaide Grey, was more than just a lovely portrait. She was more than just a beloved monarch taken too soon. Another tragic casualty of the Damaris bloodline.

She was the beginning of it all...the beginning of the adventure.

The ruby pendant, upon which hung the fate of the world, had been placed around her slender neck. It was in her veins that the first Damaris magic had sparked to life. The heart of a dragon, the fire of a queen. A woman who'd lived with a terrible secret. One that had eventually taken her life.

At least...that was the story.

"I can't believe it," Adelaide said softly, looking her up and down. "You look so much like my daughter...at first I thought it was Katerina lying in front of me. But you have your own beauty, my darling. You could only be her precious child. Everly."

The princess stared back in shock. The fae was no better. After a silent deliberation, they simultaneously concluded they were either hallucinating or dead.

Or perhaps trapped somewhere in the middle...

"I thought it was a dream," Evie finally murmured, lifting a hand once again to her head. "When we saw you in the forest, I thought it couldn't be real..."

It *couldn't* be real. She was so certain, the mere possibility had already vanished from her mind. She hadn't remembered until that very moment the lovely face that floated over them, trying to keep them conscious, murmuring words of comfort before they finally blacked out.

The motion caught Adelaide's attention and her face clouded with concern.

"Sweetheart, you shouldn't be on your feet so soon." She turned her eyes from one to the other. "And you, child. It's a miracle you didn't die from those wounds. Please, lie back down—"

"How is this possible?" Evie interrupted with a hint of caution.

She didn't want to be wary of the woman. She wanted to embrace her with both arms. But appearances could be deceiving, and the friends had been burned before. Best to stick with the facts.

And the fact was…Adelaide Grey was dead.

"You recognized me?" the queen murmured after a long silence. Her storm-cloud eyes warmed with the hint of a smile. "I was hoping you would. Surely your mother would have told you about me. But I wondered if Marcus would have removed all images of me from the castle…"

Evie stared a moment longer, then shook her head. Each answer raised more questions than before. Each sentence was more confusing than the last.

HOW was the woman standing in front of them? HOW was she still alive?

"It's a bit of a story," Adelaide continued suddenly, sensing there would be no reasoning with the children until she'd laid some of those questions to rest. "If I agree to tell it, will you let me get you some food? Perhaps check those bandages? You're still bleeding, after all."

The princess and the fae shared a quick look. Given their previous experience, both of them were half-inclined to run straight out the front door. But running wasn't what it used to be and, like it or not, they'd grown up in that castle together, looking up at the same pictures on the walls.

The woman was a living miracle. Perhaps it was time for a bit of faith.

"Start talking," Evie said quietly, offering a tentative smile. "I'll boil some water for tea…"

ONLY A FEW MINUTES later the unlikely trio was sitting around the table. There were only chairs enough for two, but that didn't seem to matter. In the excitement of seeing her long-lost granddaughter, Adelaide was completely incapable of sitting still.

She'd fretted and fussed, readjusting bandages and combing locks of hair. She'd coaxed bites of food and wiped soot off faces. She'd helped the fae limp at an excruciating speed across the room, and forced so many cups of tea the young companions were incapable of taking another sip.

Finally, when she was unable to put it off any longer, she came to a stop. Fulfilling her end of the bargain and answering all those burning questions that had plagued them since opening their eyes.

"Your grandfather didn't just send me away...he sent me away to be killed."

It was a rather explosive way to start, and Evie couldn't believe her ears.

In the years after, her mother had pieced together more of what happened. It was too much of a coincidence that soldiers had been following Adelaide in the days before her death, that before she was escorted from the garden she'd draped her magical pendant around Katerina's neck.

Between that and a diary her mother found years later at Talsing Sanctuary, it had become apparent that the king had grown wise to his wife's supernatural secret. He'd banished her from the kingdom. Sent his soldiers to make sure she'd actually left his corner of the realm.

But no one had ever gone so far as to assume he'd sentenced her to death.

"He did?" she asked quietly, feeling sick. "He actually did that?"

Adelaide hadn't said *the king*. She'd said *your grandfather*.

Evie's own bloodline had done this. Her own cursed bloodline that made her the frequent joke of her friends, but had a darker history than any of them was prepared to admit.

Ellanden glanced at her across the table, then reached below and took her hand.

"Yes, my darling, he did." Adelaide offered a sad smile before continuing. "He sent a young wizard with me, an apprentice of Alwyn's. He was one of the only sorcerers left, after Marcus' army had their fun. Rhys was supposed to be the end of me…"

Her eyes grew distant as she stared out the window.

"You see, in those days one wasn't allowed to have magic. It wasn't a gift, but a mark of execution. If a person was to show even the slightest inclination towards the mystical world, they would be sought out by the royal forces and immediately put to death. My husband made it his life's mission to exterminate anyone who showed even a touch of enchantment. Men, women, and children…it didn't matter. They were put to death all the same."

There was a slight pause.

"All the while, he didn't know one was sleeping in his bed."

She paused again, much longer this time. So long that Evie and Ellanden exchanged a quick look, wondering whether to tap her, wondering whether something wasn't quite well in her head.

Then all at once she started speaking again.

"My husband didn't know exactly what I was, only that it was a power he'd never seen. True to form, he was afraid of it. He believed he needed someone equally powerful to have me killed."

Evie nodded slowly, trying to follow along.

Rhys. Another wizard.

"Did he try?" she asked tentatively.

"No," Adelaide laughed, "and there was hardly a need. I didn't know what I was back then. I didn't know how to transform, or what I'd even transform into. The most I'd ever managed to do was conjure up a few flames, and even that could hardly be called a success."

She smiled to herself, lost in memories that had long since passed.

"The first night it happened I'd been sitting down before bed, about to comb my hair. The second I saw the flames, I remember racing to the courtyard and plunging my hands into the nearest fountain. The men and women of the court had nothing to fear from me."

Evie blushed and looked down at her hands. She remembered her mother telling a similar story. That beloved sanctuary in the mountains—she'd nearly set fire to the walls.

"And someone saw you?" Ellanden prompted cautiously. "Reported back to the king?"

He hadn't said much since the resurrected queen had returned to the cottage. Perhaps he didn't feel it was his place. Perhaps it simply required too much effort to speak.

Adelaide flashed a quick smile, but shook her head.

"No one saw me; I managed to keep it a secret a long time. The only one I finally confided in was Alwyn. It seemed a safe choice. The man was my rock. He would never betray me."

The friends shared another fleeting look.

Was it possible she still believed such a thing? Was it possible she didn't know? There wasn't a man, woman, or child in the five kingdoms who didn't know the betrayal of the wizard. How such calculated treason had shredded the very fabric of the realm. Then again, the lovely queen had recently achieved an honorary status of 'ghost'. If there was ever an excuse to be behind the times...

"Marcus wanted to kill me, but he recanted at the last moment. For whatever reason, he couldn't bear the thought of me dead. He told Rhys to imprison me instead. To protect me."

The princess shook her head. "Protect you?"

Adelaide's lips curved in a wry smile.

"Protect the realm *from* me," she corrected. "Rhys was ordered to create an enchantment, a kind of cage. Within the walls of this house, time couldn't touch us. The rest of the realm couldn't find us." Her expression darkened. "Of course, my husband took other precautions as well..."

Evie didn't know what to say to this, and felt completely overwhelmed.

How did you respond to such a story? What were you supposed to say? Adelaide Grey was dead. History had acknowledged this, a memorial had been built, the realm had mourned her loss.

And after that...the world had kept on turning.

Wars were won and lost. Kingdoms rose and fell. Some prophecies were fulfilled, while others let loose a wave of ash and ruin.

In short, time had not stopped for the fallen queen.

And Evie wasn't quite sure what to say to her now.

"So...what's changed?" Ellanden asked cautiously. "How are we able to see you? How is it that we've been allowed inside? You said the entire house was under an enchantment...?"

Adelaide froze, lost in thought. Then she lifted her head.

"The spell is broken," she said simply.

The friends tightened their grip beneath the table. In their experience, a sorcerer's spell didn't break so easily. Nor did it happen on its own. Such a thing always came with a price.

"But how is that possible?" Evie asked warily. "This Rhys...he just let you go?"

There was a sudden noise in the forest.

Evie and Ellanden pushed anxiously to their feet, but surprisingly Adelaide reacted quickest of them all. In just a split second, she'd armed herself with a flaming log pulled from the fire. Her face tensed as she gazed out to the trees, gesturing the others frantically to the stairwell.

"Quickly, children! To the topmost story!"

The friends looked at each other, then looked at the stairs.

"Why?" Evie asked anxiously, glancing again at the fae. There was no way he would be able to make such a climb. "What's coming—"

"A terrible beast," the woman said quickly. "One which I pray you never have to see. It's why Rhys and I built the house so tall, to be free from its reach. If we could just—"

But there was no more time for talking. The creature was upon them.

Granted, it probably wasn't the beast Adelaide had in mind.

"Get away from them!" Asher shouted as the door kicked open. It fell with a clatter near the stairs as he stepped menacingly into the frame. "Or I swear to the stars, I'll rip out your heart..."

Chapter 2

Growing up in a world of magic, where actual monsters prowled beneath beds and fairytale heroes leapt straight off the page, one developed a set of 'triggers'. Unspoken truths recognized by the whole of society, derived from centuries of experience—designed to keep people safe.

Blood on the moon, lock your windows until morning. The first day of harvest, beware of goblins and thieves. People who 'cried wolf' generally meant it literally. It was usually a shifter. It was usually a friend. Fairies weren't to be trusted with anything timely. Chimes of silver kept pixies away.

Screaming *vampire* was something akin to shouting the word *fire*. The only difference was that with a fire, people tended to run outside. With a vampire, they barred the doors.

The rules had been the same for generations. A single glance and Adelaide let out a wild cry.

"*Vampire!*"

Instead of bursting into movement, the room froze.

Evie was bandaged to the point of immobility. Ellanden had lost so much blood, he was rooted to the spot. The queen was as incapable of leaving the children as she was of running from a fight. And Asher...had just started to notice certain things in his kidnapping plot were amiss.

His friends had been cared for, and were in the process of drinking tea. There were flowers in the windows and the door had been unlocked as he broke it. And the woman? Their evil captor?

She looked strikingly similar to a picture he'd grown up seeing as a child.

"It can't be..." he breathed, eyes travelling between the princess and queen, both ironically frozen in the same pose. "How is this...?"

Adelaide's eyes flashed and she took a step forward. "You picked the wrong house, vampire."

For whatever reason, the voice confirmed it. Perhaps it was because she still carried the faint accent of the High Kingdom. Perhaps it was the unmistakable authority of a queen. Or perhaps it was simply because the princess had greeted him the exact same way since they were children.

He blinked in amazement, retracting the fangs at once.

"I can't believe it. You're actually—"

But the queen had no intention of talking. Nor was she going to allow the vampire to take one more step inside her house. As the others remained frozen behind her, she took a step forward.

"You're trespassing," she interrupted, throwing the flaming log back into the fire.

He startled when it crashed into the others, sending up a burst of sparks. At that point, he seemed to realize his entrance required an explanation. And perhaps a quick apology for the door.

"Forgive me." He lifted his hands with a charming smile, trying to appear as non-threatening as possible. "I meant no offense, I was just looking for my friends..."

The queen lifted her hands as well. Without the smile.

"Final warning," she breathed. "Get out of my house."

He stepped back involuntarily, hovering nervously in the frame.

"Please, you misunderstand me—"

But he never got to finish the sentence.

As fate would have it, in addition to being 'not-dead' the lovely queen wasn't nearly as dainty as she seemed. With a look of pure hatred, she let loose a wave of liquid fire.

Dragon fire. The kind of fire that only killed.

"NO!"

Evie let out a piercing scream as Ellanden dove towards Adelaide—shoving aside her pale hands with all his might. The fire took out the kitchen window instead. And most of the garden.

"He's our friend!" he was shouting. "He's not going to hurt anyone!"

The house groaned, *deeply*, an ominous backlash to the flames. In a burst of dark recognition Evie realized they were standing inside a tinder-box, that the wooden house was stacked the exact same way Belarian officials constructed funeral pyres for fallen warriors back home. She tried to make this clear in a string of nonsensical shouting, followed by another panicked scream.

But the queen was incensed.

She might have been living in a forest cottage the last fifty years, suspended in enchantment, but certain truths remained unchanged by time.

Vampires were dangerous. This one could not be allowed to live.

"Stand back!" she commanded the fae, yanking her wrists free of his grasp.

On most days, such a command would have been laughable. There were very few people in the world who could make the prince do something against his will, and most all of them were holed up in an enchanted hideaway of their own. But the guy had been recently caught in a bear-trap.

A single push and he crumpled to the ground, panting in pain and clutching his chest. At that point, Asher let out a shout of his own and rushed forward...only to meet another wave of fire.

Seven hells!

This time, he wasn't able to leap out of the way swiftly enough. He let out a sharp cry and stumbled into the table, slapping frantically at his sleeve to put out the flames.

"STOP!"

In what felt like slow motion, Evie tore across the room—sending up an explosion of jasmine tea in her wake. She leapt straight over Ellanden's body and threw herself into the line of fire, throwing up her arms as a reflection of those deadly flames danced in her eyes.

"He's the LOVE of my LIFE!"

Silence fell over the house.

The fae's eyes closed with a grimace. Adelaide's face whitened in shock. For his part Asher froze upon the table, the cuff of his sleeve still very much on fire.

Why in the WORLD did I say it like that?

Evie froze in horror, feeling like she might be sick. "I meant, he's my...my friend. *Our* friend," she clarified quickly, gesturing to Ellanden as well. "He's our friend—we grew up at the castle together."

The queen's eyebrows rose into her hair.

"At the castle?" she repeated in disbelief. "My old castle. This creature grew up there?"

Ellanden pursed his lips, torn between laughter and disapproval, while Asher stared with a fixed smile at the back of Evie's head. She blushed and avoided everyone's eyes.

"That's funny, I call him that sometimes, too..."

Seriously. What in the bloody world is actually wrong with me?

The smile behind her sharpened a bit.

"A lot's changed since you went away," she continued in a steadier voice, still positioned warily in front of her grandmother's palms. "And we can keep talking about it, but you're going to have to promise *not* to light him on fire. No matter what. I need your word on that, Adelaide."

'Grandma' would have to wait.

The woman stared at her a moment longer then lowered her hands with the hint of a smile, watching the furious blush swirling in the girl's cheeks.

"If you need my word, then you have it. Heaven forbid I set fire to your...*friend*."

Ellanden snorted with laugher as Evie silently vowed to end her own life. Only Asher was able to keep a modicum of composure. An impressive feat, considering the circumstances.

"So it's true?" He straightened up slowly, curls of smoke still rising from his shirt. "All those stories from the High Kingdom...they were a lie? You really are Adelaide Grey?"

The queen looked at him steadily, then forced a surprisingly gracious smile. "Put out your tunic, child. Your skin is burning."

Ellanden laughed out loud, then caught himself quickly. "Sorry," he murmured, trying to keep a straight face, "I'm in a lot of pain..."

The others looked at him incredulously, then froze in an awkward silence.

Considering how quickly things had escalated, time had screeched to an abrupt stop. The door was gone, the windowsill was burning, and there was no graceful conversational segue to get from an attempted daylight homicide to whatever was supposed to happen next.

The friends were at a loss. Fortunately, their hostess was not.

"How about I get some more tea?"

Despite having been missing for half a century, Adelaide Grey had played the unfortunate role of a Damaris queen for quite some time before that. It wasn't her first daylight homicide attempt. It wasn't even her second. Needless to say, she was well-versed in the script.

There was a beat of silence, then three voices chimed in all at once.

"Perfect."

"Sounds great."

"None for me...but thank you."

The queen shared a rather awkward look with the vampire then swept over to the little kitchen, patting out the flames with a rag before setting about making a floral brew.

Evie watched her for a moment, then turned back to Asher with a beaming smile.

"So...what do you think?"

"TELL ME THE TRUTH...were you bored at the fort?"

The three friends were sitting on the same sofa Ellanden had been draped across when they woke up, speaking in hushed voices as Adelaide bustled needlessly about the kitchen, giving them time to figure things out. So far, they were having trouble getting past the basics.

"Bored?" Evie repeated confusedly, thinking back on their heated night. "What do you—"

"We sneak into a heavily armed fortress and lay waste to the company of soldiers stationed there. We free the captive slaves and relocate Seth's entire village into a new home. We throw a magnificent feast and spend the first night, in longer than I can remember, safe behind stone walls."

The vampire paused a moment, looking at his friends.

"...and then you got bored, wandered off, and tried to get yourselves killed?"

They flushed and dropped their gaze, having received similar speeches before.

"It's not like it was premeditated," Ellanden muttered, fiddling with the bandages around his chest. "These things just—"

Asher slapped down his hand.

"—happen."

It was an admirable façade, but the vampire was more worried than he was letting on. The bond with the princess had led him to the clearing. The blood of the fae had drawn him inside.

"Why must you keep breaking?" he murmured, eyes sweeping over the gauze. "Why can't you manage to stay in one piece?"

"It's nothing," Ellanden said dismissively, wishing he was wearing a shirt. "A pair of slavers attacked us in the forest, then your bloody girlfriend—"

"I'm surprised you didn't find us sooner," Evie interrupted, lowering her voice to avoid any listening ears. Adelaide banged the kettle with unnecessary force in the kitchen, playing along with the charade. "...shouldn't you have come straight away?"

Asher paused a moment, then stared deliberately at his hands.

"I didn't feel anything," he said quietly, more disconcerted than he was letting on. "There was just this...blank space. But the bond is new, and when Charlotte told me you'd gone hunting I didn't think any more of it. It wasn't until a few minutes ago that I knew something was wrong."

"A few minutes?" Ellanden repeated in surprise.

"We're not far from the fortress," Asher replied, keeping his eyes on Evie. "I came as soon as I could—ran the whole way here."

She was quiet a moment, wondering if the two of them had somehow managed to screw up something as primal as a vampiric covenant. Then her face lightened in sudden understanding.

"When we were attacked, I got knocked unconscious almost immediately. You couldn't have known anything was wrong if I didn't know it myself. And we just woke up a few minutes ago."

Ellanden shook his head disapprovingly. "Still...shoddy intuition, if you ask me."

"No one did," Asher replied coolly, but he was visibly relieved—having spent the entire day missing his girlfriend and worrying about the bond himself.

With a sudden smile he laced his fingers with Evie's, trailing them lightly along the side of her hand. She heated with an immediate flush, surprised that his skin was warm as well. He was usually so cold. When they slept outside, she tended to keep a cloak between them.

Not always...

Her cheeks darkened as she thought again about what they'd done the night before. So much had happened in between, it already felt like a lifetime ago. Yet she could remember each moment with perfect clarity. The way he caught his breath when she climbed on top of him, fiery hair blowing across his chest. The way his hands wrapped around the small of her back, bringing them even closer together. The little smile that crept up the side of his face—

"So, uh...what happened to your head?"

Those warm feelings vanished on a dime.

"...what?"

He gestured with an apologetic grimace.

"Your...uh...it's barely noticeable..."

With a feeling of dread she heaved herself towards the window, then jerked back almost immediately when she caught sight of her reflection. It didn't look human. There was a face, sure enough, but the rest had been layered in such a thick blanket of gauze and medicinal herbs it was a small miracle her neck was managing to keep the whole thing upright.

She let out a yelp, then turned a scathing glare onto Ellanden. "All this time...you didn't want to tell me?"

He shrugged. "I got used to it."

There was a quiet humming from the kitchen. The three of them turned to watch Adelaide brewing another batch of tea, a beatific smile lighting the edges of her face.

*All this time...*Evie thought, staring in silence, *I could have known her. She could have known me.*

"I should hug her," she murmured, turning to the boys. "She's my grandmother, back from the dead. I should give her a hug, right? You'd give her a hug?"

Ellanden shook his head briskly. "Fae don't hug. We embrace."

There was a pause.

"Is that, like...a sex thing?"

"Not always."

"Could you two keep it together for a single minute?" Asher interrupted, trying to rein in his exasperation. "*What* is she doing here? How is she possibly still...you know..."

"Alive?"

The three looked up with a start as Adelaide joined them, balancing a tray for tea. She set it on the table before settling beside them with a little smile.

"Funny you should ask..."

Ellanden cast a quick look at the vampire.

"She was just telling us. Then you kicked down the door."

Asher tensed apologetically, but Evie took his hand.

"The story the castle told was a lie," she explained quietly. "There was no riding accident in the woods, and the funeral was a fake. After my grandfather discovered Adelaide had powers he exiled her from the kingdom, sending a wizard along to keep her trapped in this cottage under a spell."

Asher's lips parted in surprise, but the friends had a strange history and one learned to take these things in stride. But there was no preparing for what the queen said next.

"And after a few years...we fell in love."

The friends froze in astonishment, then edged closer on their chairs.

"You fell in love?" Evie repeated in disbelief. "With a wizard?"

The queen's eyes twinkled with a smile.

"I think you'll find that people find love in the most unlikely of places, Everly. And with the most unlikely of creatures..." She let that sink in a moment, then gave them a little wink. "At any rate, Rhys wasn't a wizard like the ones you're picturing. He was young, he was kind. We'd known each other at the castle, before everything started falling apart. Sometimes I wonder, if I'd confided my secret to him instead of Alwyn how different things might have been..."

The princess went suddenly rigid, replaying the words in her mind.

No one saw her that night, no one knew she had powers. No one except Alwyn.

And then suddenly...the king.

"So you know about Alwyn?" she asked tentatively. She'd been debating whether or not to bring it up. "You know about the prophecy? How he tried to steal my mother's power?"

Adelaide nodded briskly, bowing her head.

"Yes," she said softly, "I know all that."

It seemed too much for her to talk about, but the princess was still forced to ask.

"...how?"

The woman had been locked in an enchanted cottage for almost fifty years. The man charged with keeping her there had been locked inside as well. There was no contact with the outside world, there had been no pardon or reprieve.

How was it possible she knew anything? How was it possible the three friends were even sitting there, crowded together on the little couch?

Adelaide flashed a sudden look. A guarded look. One that sent chills up Evie's spine. This story didn't have a happy ending. How many of their stories ever did?

"When I first came here, all those years ago...it nearly broke me. And it wasn't the loss of my home or my crown. It wasn't the loss of my husband, or even the knowledge that every silent misery had come at his hand. It was my children. My precious children. I knew that I'd—" She caught her breath suddenly, as if she'd received a slap. "I'd never see them again."

The room fell silent as she took a moment to collect herself, staring out the window with an expression Evie had never seen. It went beyond sadness. There were no more tears left to cry.

"There were times when I begged Rhys to kill me," she murmured. "What was the point of living if I couldn't have them? I paced the halls day and night, staring into the garden, seeing those two little faces..." She paused again, then forced herself through. "The years went past and it never got easier. There isn't a way to lessen that kind of pain. But things were changing between me and Rhys. There were days I'd catch myself smiling. There were times he could make me laugh."

She shivered suddenly, then glanced briefly over the room.

"He was the one who encouraged me to paint."

Evie twisted around to follow her gaze, staring at the portraits hanging on the walls. They were the first things she noticed upon opening her eyes—the first thing she forgot upon waking.

Such familiar faces. Ones she'd known her entire life.

My family.

With a look of wonder she pushed to her feet and walked across the room, pausing in front of a fire-haired girl with large, inquisitive eyes. Even so young there was no mistaking that lovely face, any more than the dark-haired boy beside her. The one with the hounds curled at his feet.

"It was the only way I could see them," Adelaide said softly. "My beautiful children...it was the only way I could keep them with me."

A wistful smile pulled the corners of Evie's mouth as she lifted the tips of her fingers to touch her mother's cheek. Sometimes, it felt like a few weeks. Sometimes, it felt like years. And sometimes, it felt like an entire lifetime she'd been away, longing for the warmth of those arms.

But it wasn't the only picture on the wall. There were others hanging beside it.

"This is Rhys?" she asked softly, staring up at him.

He was young, like Adelaide had said. No older than the queen was herself. And he was handsome. Not in a conventional way, perhaps. There was a lack of symmetry to his face that made her question the brushstrokes. But he'd been gifted with one of those contagious smiles, and those dark eyes teemed with the kind of mischief that might have made it very easy to fall in love.

She took a step closer, then glanced down at a frame that had fallen to the floor.

"Who's this?"

It was another young boy, but this one didn't look like her uncle. He had the same dark hair as Kailas, but there was something different about the eyes. Something different about the mouth, too. It thinned towards the edges, like it was hovering on the edge of a sneer.

In her periphery, Adelaide went suddenly still.

"That's Kaleb...my son."

Evie almost dropped the picture.

What?!

"You had another son?" she asked in astonishment, staring back at the child. "But how is that possible? If the king was already..."

She trailed off, feeling suddenly foolish.

Oh. Right.

Her fingers tightened along the edges of the frame as another obvious realization shook her to the core. If this man was Adelaide's son...he was Katerina's half-brother. He was her uncle.

She stared back down at the picture.

Maybe it isn't a sneer. Maybe it's a strange smile.

"But Everly, there's more," Adelaide said in a sudden rush, wincing slightly as if it pained her to look at the painting straight on. "There's a reason the spell was broken. There's a reason we found each other in the forest. Kaleb wasn't a part of the enchantment. He was born after his father cast the spell. He was able to come and go as he pleased. He was able to live in the real world."

Evie shook her head blankly as the boys pushed slowly to their feet.

"The real world," she repeated blankly. "Then why didn't he...why are you talking about him like that?" A wave of inexplicable dread washed over her. "Is he all right? Did something..."

Looking back on it later, she'd never be able to explain how she suddenly knew. How in that one moment, staring down at her grandmother's painting, it all clicked into place.

A man with the power of a wizard. A man with the heart of a dragon.

A man born in the shadows with nothing to lose.

Kaleb Grey...it's been you the whole time.

Chapter 3

"I dreamt of him, you know." Evie stood at the window, staring out at the fiery remains of the garden. "I've never seen his face, but he's been in my dreams..."

Standing in the kitchen behind her, the men exchanged a quick look.

They'd watched in silence as the princess studied the portrait, discovering an uncle she never knew she had. They hadn't understood how she'd made the connection between the dark-eyed boy and the phantom they'd been racing—the one hell-bent on destroying the world with a cursed stone.

They'd expected Adelaide to deny it. For her to laugh at the idea, then offer a reasonable explanation instead. But she'd lingered only a moment, then fled up the stairs.

She'd taken the picture with her.

They'd had a thousand questions, a thousand concerns. But looking at Evie now, staring out the same dreary window her grandmother had for years, they were at a complete loss for words.

"Say something," Ellanden breathed, soft enough that only the vampire would hear. "This is when you're supposed to say something—to fix it."

Asher glanced at him before turning back to the princess.

What could he say? How could it be fixed? When the man they'd been chasing the last ten years, the man ripping the five kingdoms apart at the seams, was her own flesh and blood.

"You dreamt of him?" he repeated softly, coming to stand behind her. Both hands rested tentatively on her shoulders, relieved when she didn't pull away. "But you've never seen his face?"

She stared blankly out the window, eyes fixed on the trees.

"He wasn't a man. He was a dragon." A belated shiver shook her shoulders, catching in the vampire's hands. "A dragon more deadly and powerful than any I've ever seen."

A heavy silence blanketed the room.

There weren't many responses to such a declaration, and nerves had already been stretched well past the breaking point. Ellanden was still reeling from the slavers, Asher was still reeling from the shock of waking up to find his girlfriend missing, and Evie was still staring out the window. Lost in a daze.

After a few minutes, the vampire asked the inevitable question.

"…what did the dragon do?'

At this point, it hardly mattered. A dragon with the powers of a sorcerer had sided against them in a race to find a cursed rock. There ceased to be degrees of calamity to that sort of thing.

But Evie couldn't help but answer, the images looping through her mind.

"It told me how we were going to be too late, how we were looking in the wrong place." She paused ever so slightly. "How we didn't stand a chance of stopping him."

No need to share how she'd agreed completely in the moment. It was already written all over her face. Instead she took a deep breath, turning away from the window.

"There were other voices, trying to warn me. But I was never able to find out who they were. Even with my vision quest at the Kreo camp, there were never any people. Just…darkness."

Another silence fell between them. Even more charged than the last.

"And you didn't think to tell us?" Ellanden asked, trying to keep the anger from his voice.

"They were dreams," Evie said flatly. "We all have dreams."

Asher stayed quiet, staring deep into her eyes.

"Not like that," the fae protested, pushing to his feet. "Everly, you can't keep things like that to yourself. The stakes couldn't be higher, there's no telling what might be important—"

"I saw you all dead," she interrupted, "floating in a sea of bones. I saw the beast flying towards the High Kingdom to set my mother's castle on fire. It was bigger than this house. Big enough to set the entire forest ablaze with a single breath."

She turned back to the window, staring at the trees.

"I just didn't know his name was Kaleb..."

The fae stood behind her a moment, as if waiting for something more before lifting a hand to his chest and slumping suddenly into the nearest chair. His face was drawn and his skin pale.

"I take it back," he murmured. "In the future, keep those things to yourself."

Asher stood there silently, staring at the back of her head.

"Is that all?" he asked softly.

She stiffened in spite of herself. "Isn't that enough?"

He took a step closer, turning her gently to face him. "You didn't see anything...happen?"

His dark eyes latched onto hers, shining with an emotion she didn't understand. Or maybe she did understand it. Maybe she just wanted to hear him say it out loud.

"Like what?' she asked, almost coldly. "Did I see myself *die*?"

The word scorched the air and he took a step back, not a shred of emotion on his face.

Unfortunately, that was no longer enough. She could feel the cold panic with every pounding beat of his heart. Just like he could feel her own, tightening like a noose around his neck.

"Would I really be the first of us to have that dream?" she challenged quietly, looking at each of them in turn. "Am I really the only one thinking of it?"

Both men froze in perfect unison before suddenly avoiding her gaze.

No, don't be shy.

She focused on Ellanden first, grabbing him by the sleeve and yanking him to his feet.

"You've thrown yourself off every ledge and into the path of every danger we've stumbled upon since leaving the royal caravan. You shoot at things first, make them notice you first. You saved my life with the vampires. You offered to stay in Cosette's place."

She hurled each one like a dagger. Like they weren't mere acts of bravery. Like there was something bizarrely self-serving in them as well. To prove her point further, she flicked his bandage.

"Ash is right. You keep breaking. But that's your plan, isn't it?" she accused softly. "To be the one the prophecy doomed to fail. To be the one who takes the fall."

He grimaced when she touched him, then pulled away—flushed and silent. At one point he opened his mouth to speak, then turned deliberately to the window, staring out at the trees.

She nodded with grim satisfaction before turning to Asher.

"And you..."

This one was harder. There were tears in her eyes. Instead of speech-making, she quoted his own words right back to him. The silent prayer he'd murmured while kneeling by Ellanden's side.

"It's not supposed to be you. You have to keep going. It's supposed to be me." She took a step closer, staring up at him, shaking her head. "You're no better than the fae—planning in secret, biding your time. And you have the nerve to ask if *I've* seen something?"

He held her gaze, never backing down.

"I can't lose you," he said quietly. "I can't lose either of you. I won't apologize for that."

If they'd had the discussion even a day before, things might have been different. If they hadn't completed a bond that provided open access to each other's hearts and minds.

She used that bond like a weapon, staring deep into his eyes.

"And do you think I could survive something like that?"

It was as if she never actually experienced the emotion. Instead of feeling it, she merely watched it play out across his face. A ragged devastation, like he'd clutched a sharpened blade.

"Enough of this," Ellanden commanded suddenly, turning away from the trees. "It won't do any good to bicker amongst ourselves. We've ignored that line of the prophecy from the first night we got it, and we won't let it govern us now. If one of us is fated to die before the end, then it's already been written. Nothing we do can affect a change."

The others flashed him a look, but nodded numbly. Sometimes amidst those moments of fantastical impulsivity, the fae was surprisingly sane.

"So you have a grandmother...and an uncle." He studied Evie carefully, gauging how she reacted to each one. "What we need is to find out everything that can help us, and get back to the others. If this man is as powerful as you say...there isn't a lot of time."

"I can help with that."

The friends looked over with a start as Adelaide appeared on the stairs. Her eyes were red, but it didn't look like she'd been crying. Whatever tears she had for her youngest son had been spent long ago. She took a step forward, squaring her shoulders with determination.

"This prophecy...it wouldn't have something to do with a missing stone would it?"

Evie stiffened in spite of herself, staring across the room.

The woman had been through hell. She'd lost her family, lost her home. She was a good person—that much the princess knew. But this was her *child*. Would she really work against him?

"What makes you think that?" Asher asked cautiously.

The queen studied him a moment, then sat down at the table. After a few seconds the others gathered around her, pulling up extra chairs.

"You asked me before how this was possible," she murmured, glancing at Ellanden. "How you'd be able to set foot in an enchanted house. I told you the spell had broken—but there's more to it than that. We were forced to break the spell, Rhys and I. We couldn't continue on with our lives, knowing what Kaleb wanted. Knowing what he was planning to do."

She paused under the weight of their gazes, shaking her head with remorse.

"You have to understand...he wasn't always the way he is now. He was a good child, a sweet child. In many ways, he reminded me a lot of your mother." She glanced at Evie with the hint of a smile before bowing her head. "But that was the problem. He wasn't your mother. She and Kailas were living at the castle, heirs to the High Kingdom...while he was stuck in a hovel in the woods."

There was something surprisingly depressing about the way she said it. Something that made Evie feel the need to defend the eclectic little cottage.

"It isn't so bad," she interjected, glancing up the unending stairwell. "At any rate, it wasn't always roses for my mother and Kailas. Nor was it lacking in spells..."

A flash of dark anger shot across Adelaide's face and she pulled in a steadying breath.

"So I've heard...from Kaleb, as fate would have it. And he didn't always hate it here. When he was a child, he used to spend hours playing with me in the garden. He loved to take walks along the edge of the forest. He loved to read..."

She trailed off, glancing at a shelf of books alongside the fireplace.

Despite the tidiness of the rest of the house, this looked as though it had been deliberately neglected—much like the forgotten portrait the princess had gathered off the floor.

"Fairytales," Evie said with surprise, looking at some of the names. Ironically enough, many were copies of the same books in her own nursery. "My mother used to read me these."

Adelaide smiled again, and this time it lingered in her eyes.

"I'm not surprised; they were always Katy's favorites. When Kaleb brought them home one day, I wondered how they might have..." She shook her head. "But that's neither here nor there. He soon moved past them, taking interest in other things."

Sure enough, there were other books on that shelf. Darker books. The kind the castle would never have kept in the library. Full of terrible creatures, black magic, and spells.

"It tortured him, you see. He'd go down to the village—hear the locals gossiping about what was happening at the castle. For better or worse, Damaris blood ruled these kingdoms for nearly five centuries. Your mother and uncle were at the heart of that. He was living in the woods."

She let out a quiet sigh, turning reflexively to the window.

"He started spending more and more time away, going off on longer trips on his own. Rhys and I tried to stop it. We cautioned him about what might happen if he were discovered, if it was discovered that we'd had a child. But by the end...I don't think he even cared. It's like he wanted someone to find out. If only for something new to happen. If only for a change."

Her eyes lifted and her body went very still.

"And then one day...he didn't come back at all."

Evie leaned back with a start, struck by the sudden end to the story. She'd been expecting explosive arguments, pleading and tears. Maybe a little duel between the wizards.

"He just left?" she prompted quietly. "Without a word of goodbye?"

Adelaide nodded slowly, her eyes glued to those trees. As if she could see him walking away, as if she was still waiting for him to come back. All at once, despite the timeless enchantment, she looked very old.

"It wasn't until years later that I saw him again, and even then it was just to look through his father's books. He was a different man than the one I remembered. So full of anger, so full of hate."

"But why?" Evie asked incredulously, still uncertain of the timeline. "He was angry about the magical integration? Or about my uncle's spell? The king had died years before...why didn't he just go to the castle and tell everyone who he was? They were his family."

Her grandmother smiled sadly.

"Because he didn't want another family, my dear. He wanted to rule." She pulled in a deep breath, laying the last of the cards on the table. "He'd gone to the library at Harenthall, learned all about your parents, learned all about the prophecy they'd been destined to fulfill. When he came back, he was a changed person. He didn't laugh, didn't smile. He didn't have time for anything except those damn books. Always reading, always talking about a dark stone."

Ellanden glanced up suddenly, a peculiar look on his face. "And when was that?"

"I'm sorry?" Adelaide asked.

"When did he come back?"

She thought about it a moment.

"It couldn't have been more than ten years ago. Your parents had just thrown a great party, celebrating the anniversary of their victory at the Battle of the Dunes. He'd gone to the castle, he admitted to us later. I was so afraid he'd do something terrible. But he said his plans had changed."

The friends went suddenly still, freezing in a crescent around the table. He'd been there at the party? The night they got the prophecy...he'd actually been wandering the grounds?

Evie's face went pale.

He poisoned the wine.

"When he left again, I wasn't surprised," Adelaide continued obliviously. "Rhys tried to stop him, but his powers had already far exceeded our own. We had hoped that he'd let it go, that if he spent enough time in the world he'd give up his vendetta and live the rest of his life in peace. But when he came back a few weeks ago...we knew it wasn't meant to be."

"A few weeks ago?" Evie repeated breathlessly, poised on the edge of her seat.

"I'd never seen him like that—he was manic. Kept muttering something about a shipwreck, how there was a huge storm. We pressed and pressed, until eventually he lost his temper. He told us about the prophecy, how the three of you were after the stone. When he told us why *he* wanted it, the things he planned to do...we knew we had to warn you. But we were trapped in this house."

The princess shook her head slowly, trying to follow along.

"But why were you still here?" she asked. "Why didn't you leave sooner? Once the king had died...why didn't you just come back?"

Adelaide bowed her head.

"We couldn't," she said simply. "I loved Rhys. And there's only one way to break a spell."

...loved Rhys.

"But you said the spell is broken now," Evie repeated in confusion. "How did you...?"

She trailed off, feeling suddenly cold.

"Where is Rhys?"

※

THE TRIO OF FRIENDS stood beside Adelaide, staring down at the grave.

It was a tiny plot, just at the edge of the garden, unadorned and surrounded in a such a lovely grove of flowers you'd never know it was there until you were standing right in front of it.

"He did it himself." Adelaide clutched a hand to her stomach, staring down at the freshly-turned dirt. "I was supposed to be there with him; I promised I wouldn't make him die alone. But he didn't want to put me through that. He ate some hemlock. Picked it right here in the garden."

Evie looked around at the flowers, wondering why they grew hemlock at all.

"He was always protecting me, my Rhys," the queen continued softly. "Ever since we left the castle. Even before—at the risk of angering the king. And then again, just a few days ago. The man gave everything he had, sacrificing his life to save a group of people he never knew."

The friends stood in silence, not knowing what to say.

"When you found us in the woods?" Evie finally ventured.

Adelaide nodded, tightening her shawl with a quick breath.

"I was coming to find you. To be honest, I didn't think it would happen. I had no idea where to look. Then when I saw that burst of fire...it was like the stars had finally aligned."

It only took ten years.

"He was a brave man," Asher said softly. "The entire realm owes him a great deal."

Ellanden nodded slowly, staring at the queen.

"I swear to you, we'll do everything we can to honor his memory. Even if it—" He cut off suddenly, taking a step for balance. "Even if it means—"

Another step. The ground was shaking.

"What is that?" Evie cried in alarm, searching instinctively for a pack of wild hyenas. "Some kind of earthquake?"

Adelaide closed her eyes with a weary sigh.

"No, my dear. I'm afraid it's nothing so simple."

A sudden bellow shook the woods and flocks of birds exploded from the trees, screeching loudly as they scattered in the sky. The friends stood paralyzed in the garden.

Then Ellanden turned to the queen with a hint of dread. "...you mentioned a beast?"

Chapter 4

"There's no need to panic."

The trio of friends had backed slowly into the house, eyes on the forest. The queen had followed along, shutting the door quickly behind them. A second later, she bolted it with a large plank that had been leaning against the wall. When that was finished, she bolted it yet again.

"Oh good," Evie said faintly, feeling a bit light-headed, "there *isn't* some nightmarish monster coming to kill us?"

Adelaide flashed her a quick look. "...define monster."

The ground trembled again, shaking the walls of the house.

Seven hells...we're all going to die.

"What is it?" Asher said shortly, eyes on the trees. "What's coming?"

The second he asked the question the friends started scrolling through a list of possibilities in their minds, glancing about the house for anything they could use as a weapon.

There weren't many options and they weren't exactly at their best.

Ellanden was still bandaged around the ribs but he picked up the fire-poker, eyeing the tree-line. Evie and Asher took up position beside him, armed with an empty teacup and a set of fangs. They stood there quietly a moment, then the vampire shot her a sideways glance.

"You remember that you can shoot fire, right?"

She blushed furiously and set down the cup.

"There won't be any need for that," Adelaide said quickly. Unlike the others, she had forsaken the concept of weapons entirely and was rummaging in the kitchen cabinets. After a moment, she pulled out a dried bouquet of purple flowers. "This should do the trick."

The friends blinked at her, wondering if she'd been out in the woods too long.

"I don't understand," Ellanden finally managed. "Are you courting the beast?"

The queen bristled at the term, but maintained a neutral expression.

"My husband may have banished me from the kingdom, but he couldn't put his trust entirely in a sorcerer without taking other precautions as well. Before we left, he forced Rhys to summon a creature to guard the cottage. That way, even if the enchantment failed and I managed to get out, I'd never make it through the forest."

Evie nodded slowly, fearing the worst. "And this creature...?"

The footsteps were getting louder, each one heavy enough to rattle the walls. At any moment the beast was going to burst through the trees, but still the queen hesitated.

"Creature is a rather strong word. I wouldn't—"

In hindsight, it probably was better that she didn't tell them. It was one of those words that should be avoided saying out loud. At any rate, it wasn't like there was a way to temper the shock.

The moment it crashed out of the trees, the trio stepped back in unison.

...that's an ogre.

There was no mistaking such a creature and there was no tearing your eyes away. Evie had seen one only once before, when they were standing outside the arena in Tarnaq. Even amidst such a crowd, it had earned a permanent place in her memory. This one was much bigger than that.

"That's impossible," Asher breathed, taking another step back. "How is it so...?"

BIG.

They were supposed to be big. They were known for being big. But this one took it to a whole different level. Its bristly forehead grazed the tops of the trees.

"They never stop growing," Adelaide said softly, gazing up at the creature with a peculiar expression in her eyes. "As long as they're alive, they'll continue to grow. But most of them live violently and die off before... It's why this house is so tall. We kept adding on new levels."

Evie cast her a lingering look, finding this hardly comforting. "So why exactly aren't you screaming—"

"Because there's no need to panic."

The princess sucked in a quick breath as the windows rattled.

"You're running out of those."

"Said the girl who fell in love with a vampire," Adelaide answered evenly before flashing Asher a quick smile. "No offense, darling. You seem lovely."

He ran his tongue nervously over his fangs. "...thanks."

"As for the ogre, there's no need for a fight." The queen tightened her grip on the flowers, squaring her shoulders as she stepped towards the door. "The valerian will put him right to sleep—"

No fewer than three people yanked her back.

"Are you crazy?!" Evie hissed, ducking out of sight as the beast stared suspiciously at the house. "That thing would crush you in a second!"

"He won't do that," Adelaide said patiently, pulling herself free. "If you can just—"

"I don't see why this is complicated," Asher interjected, picking up a wooden bureau to wedge against the door. "Nor do I understand why it's been permitted to grow so large. You can shoot *fire*. Why didn't you just...you know?"

"Incinerate it," Ellanden finished unfeelingly.

Both friends threw him a strained look, while the queen flushed with guilt.

"Up until recently, I didn't have the option. I told you of the enchantment; both Rhys and I were tied to this property. There was no way to fight such a creature if I couldn't leave the garden."

Evie looked at her cautiously, sensing there was more.

"And once the enchantment broke?"

Again the queen hesitated, glancing reflexively towards the woods.

"The thing is...for almost fifty years there's just been the three of us..." She twisted her fingers together, unable to look any of them in the eye. "You start to get used to such things, and I just couldn't...I couldn't bring myself to..."

The friends stared back in disbelief.

History books be damned. The legend herself, famed Queen of the High Kingdom, was angled protectively in front of an ogre. Wringing her hands like it was some kind of beloved pet.

"Tell me honestly," Evie began slowly, "...have you named it?"

The queen flushed and avoided the question.

"I don't see how that's relevant," she said briskly, pacing again towards the door. "And at any rate, there's no need to destroy it now. I'll just give it the flowers like I always do—"

Ellanden caught her arm, stepping in between.

"No need to destroy it?" he repeated gently, staring into her eyes. "Your Majesty...you said yourself the enchantment is broken. The beast is no longer bound to you, to this place. As soon as it realizes this it will expand its hunting grounds, behaving as all ogres do—searching for the nearest food source. And that food source happens to be a settlement of some very close friends of ours."

Evie glanced at him in surprise before turning back with a belated kind of dread. She hadn't yet put the two together. All those people they'd relocated, Seth's entire village, were just a few minutes' run from the cottage. There was no way the ogre would miss them. And secure as the fort was, she didn't think the creature would have the slightest bit of trouble with the moat.

"We can't allow such a thing to happen," the fae continued gently. "As familiar as the beast has become...we cannot allow it to roam free."

Adelaide may have had decades of experience and wisdom on her side, but she found herself trapped by the simple truth of this statement. Her eyes travelled once more out the window, resting a moment on the dreadful brute before her shoulders fell with a quiet sigh.

"You're right," she said softly, setting down the valerian. "I'm sorry, I was just..." She shook her head quickly, tightening her shawl. "I'll go take care of it—"

This time, it was Evie who stopped her.

"You'll do nothing of the sort. Let us take care of the ogre. At this point, the sight of you would only excite it. We'll create a distraction, give you time to slip away into the woods."

The queen looked at her in surprise before her eyes drifted to the young men standing beside her. One of them was wearing only half a shirt—the rest had been burned off his skin by dragon-fire. The other was now using the fire-poker as a sort of cane, helping him balance while he breathed through the pain radiating from the vicious wound on his chest. The princess herself was still sporting an odd sort of medicinal turban. All of them were young. Very, *very* young.

Evie flushed beneath her gaze, unrolling the bandages quickly from her head. "We've done this kind of thing before."

Adelaide pursed her lips, nodding slowly. "I'm sure you have," she said kindly. "And I'm sure you're very good at it. But if you think I'm going to let my only granddaughter throw herself in the path of such a creature—"

"Carpathians, kelpies, vampires, giants," Evie interrupted sharply. Delighted as she was to have met the woman, she wasn't about to take orders from someone who'd spent the better part of a century living in a vegetable patch. "And that's not even mentioning the basilisk."

Her eyes burned into Adelaide's with quiet intensity, refusing to back down.

"I am not a child. I *have* done this kind of thing before. And if you think I'm going to let my only *grandmother* throw herself in the path of such a creature...you've absolutely lost your mind."

The two women stared at each other for a suspended moment, then the queen's lips curved up with the hint of a smile.

"Your mother's daughter, through and through."

Deciding to take this as permission Evie gestured upstairs quickly, feeling suddenly pressed for time. The only thing keeping the ogre at bay was its lingering confusion as the enchantment continued to fade. But if Adelaide could leave the property, then the beast could most certainly set foot inside. The second it realized this, they would have just seconds before it decided to attack.

"Do you want to bring anything with you?" she asked swiftly, glancing at the portraits still hanging on the wall. "I can't imagine you'll come back to this house."

In a few minutes, I can't imagine this house will still be standing.

Much to her surprise, the queen shook her head.

"This isn't my home anymore. All the people who made it a home are gone." She cast a final look around before surprising the princess further by pulling her into a sudden embrace. "We're together now, my darling. It's time to turn the page."

Evie tensed in spite of herself then lay her hands on the woman's back, leaning closer for a discreet sniff of her hair. Jasmine and paint. And something she hoped very much wasn't hemlock.

"I just found you," Adelaide breathed, tightening her grip as her eyes closed shut. "Promise me that I won't lose you all over again."

A dull pain throbbed in the princess' chest. She heard so much of her mother in those words, in that voice. Her own eyes opened in a cloud of crimson hair.

"I promise."

Adelaide pulled back with a twinkling smile. "That means letting your friends take the brunt of it," she whispered conspiratorially.

The men laughed obligingly, bracing for what was to come.

"Where shall we meet you?" Ellanden asked, glancing every few seconds at the window.

"The road where I found you is just a mile or so to the east. I'll wait for you there. You really can't miss it," she added with another smile. "Half the mountain burned to the ground."

The men glanced back at Evie, who occupied herself swiftly with the teacup.

"I'll see you soon, my darlings. Good luck with Clancy."

The vampire looked up slowly.

"Who's—"

But the door opened and they were suddenly out of time.

As it turned out, there was no need to create a distraction. The ogre had grown as accustomed to the captive queen as she was to him. It hardly spared her a second glance as she slipped away into the trees. It was far more preoccupied with the three friends left standing on the porch.

There was a moment where time seemed to freeze.

They looked at the ogre. The ogre looked at them.

"Clancy?" Ellanden quoted, with the trace of a grin.

Asher shook his head with a long-suffering sigh.

"She's *definitely* your grandmother."

EVIE EXPECTED IT TO happen quickly, as these things so often did. A blitz attack that would leave some if not all of them dead. But whether it was the lingering enchantment, the shock of seeing three brand new faces, or simply the fact that it wasn't yet hungry, the beast just stood at the tree-line—staring up towards the house. For a while, the friends had debated launching a blitz attack of their own. But while they might joke about those masochistic impulses, it would take a special kind of insanity to willingly charge an ogre. So they went back inside and proceeded to wait.

"He's not moving."

The three friends sat with their backs to the door, mentally calculating how long it would take a magically-befuddled ogre to venture across property lines. At least, that's what they were supposed to be doing. Two of them were sitting. One of them kept sneaking looks out the window.

"Did you hear me?" Ellanden repeated impatiently. "I said he's *not* moving."

Evie stared vacantly at the paintings, while Asher banged his head against the wood.

"You know what, Ellanden? It's extraordinary—given that I'm sitting just a few inches away from you—but I actually *did* hear you say that about ten or twelve times."

"...that he's not moving?"

"I'm going to strangle you."

"I can't believe she didn't take anything," Evie murmured. "Decades she's lived in this place, but when it's time to leave...she just walks out the door."

Asher turned from the fae to the princess.

"You heard what she said...this isn't a home without the people she loved and lost. But she has that again," he added softly. "She has a chance at a new family...with you."

Evie nodded slowly, still feeling the warmth of that hug.

"He's just *standing* there."

The vampire gritted his teeth and turned back to the fae. "Landi—"

"I'm just saying, the thing hasn't moved since Evie's demented grandmother slipped off into the trees." He shifted uneasily, then stretched up for another look. "Maybe we should provoke it—"

"Would you stop?" Asher demanded, yanking him back down. "I know that happens to be your specialty, but to charge such a beast is madness. We have to let it come to us. It'll happen soon enough. Then you can provoke the thing all you like."

Ellanden nodded distractedly, then stretched up once again. "I'm just going to check..."

"How am I supposed to tell people?" Evie murmured, peering up at the cherubic faces of her mother and uncle. "For centuries the Damaris bloodline has been a plague upon the realm. The villain in almost every story." She shook her head slowly, trapped in that fixed gaze. "How am I supposed to tell people that it's happening all over again?"

Asher's lips parted, but he didn't know what to say.

It didn't help that they'd been pinned down by an ogre—a leftover remnant of a Damaris spell. It also didn't help that he was feeling every heartbreak on his girlfriend's lovely face.

"Technically, he's not a Damaris," Ellanden said helpfully. "Technically, he's a Grey."

The princess looked at him incredulously. The vampire counted slowly back from ten.

"But your mother," Asher finally managed, reaching down to take her hand, "your mother changed all of that. She brought the kingdoms back together. Redeemed your family name."

Evie glanced down at their fingers, but her eyes were cold.

"And what about me?" she muttered under her breath. "I decide to duck into some lunatic's circus tent and the entire thing falls apart."

There was a pause.

"Maybe it's asleep."

The couple turned at the same time towards the fae. He was still straining up as much as his recent injury would allow, peering through the window with a hand braced against his chest.

After a few seconds, he turned expectantly to Asher.

"Do ogres sleep with their eyes open?"

The vampire sat there a moment, then nodded.

"Yes."

Back to the princess.

"Sweetheart...your mother saved the realm. Your uncle saved the realm. And in a lunatic's circus tent, you were given a prophecy to save the realm yourself." He squeezed her hand, but she refused to look at him. He kept squeezing until she lifted her eyes. "That was Damaris blood, too."

She stared at him for a long time, then her lips curved with the hint of a smile.

"I'm sorry my grandmother called you a creature. And, you know...for the fire."

He stretched out his wrists with a grimace, leaning back against the door.

"That's all right. I'm sure it's nothing less than what your mother will do herself." He paled at the thought. "And that's not even considering your father..."

Her eyes shot up immediately, widening to half of her face.

"My *mother*," she breathed, putting it together for the first time. "How is she possibly going to react to any of this? It's bad enough she thinks her only daughter was killed. Now I'm going to show up with her long-departed mother?"

Ellanden went very still beside them. "Hey, guys?"

Asher waved him silent, pushing back her hair with a smile. "I'm betting on a subdued reaction."

Evie laughed in spite of herself. "From *my* mother? Subdued?"

"You guys?"

Asher leaned back with a grin. "You know...minimal casualties, some inconsequential property damage. If we're very lucky, she won't take flight—"

"*It moved.*"

Chapter 5

Ten minutes later the friends were crouched in what used to be the old tool shed, watching as the queen's pet ogre trampled what remained of the garden outside the house. They had launched what could best be described as a pre-emptive attack before swiftly deciding their chances of staying alive would be better served by hiding amidst the rakes and shrubbery.

It had been a relatively easy decision.

The second the beast realized that Adelaide was no longer in the cottage, it had decided to dismember whoever remained. It had demonstrated this strategy by yanking the iron-work furnace right out of the wall and tearing it apart, piece by piece. The friends had watched in silence, jumping as the final piece clattered to the ground. Then they'd turned on their heels and sprinted outside.

"This is why they planted the hemlock," Evie murmured, watching the cheerful rampage through a crack in the wood. "I was wondering why they even had it...but it was in case Clancy went crazy and did something like this."

Already it was a miracle the beast hadn't accidentally consumed enough to do itself harm, given the way it was tearing through the herbs. If it wasn't for the fact that it had been momentarily distracted by a tiny bird feeder, there was a chance it would have eaten everything in sight.

Ellanden threw her a quick glance before turning back to the garden.

"Don't call it Clancy." He flinched as a wave of crushed turnips struck the dilapidated shed, glancing at the vampire. "And *you*—would you stop fidgeting? You'll give away our position."

Asher massaged his hand, glaring in the dark. "Landi, I could start singing Becatti showtunes and it still wouldn't give away our position. The thing has no idea we're here."

Strange as it sounded, that was probably true.

A distant cousin of giants, ogres were massive in size but possessed the brain power of small children—strangers to such concepts as 'object permanence' and 'restraint'. The second the friends left its line of sight, they had effectively vanished from its mind. Of course, that was all subject to change. And in another twist of irony, the beast seemed partial to showtunes itself.

A discordant humming echoed from the far side of the garden as it made its way slowly through a patch of carrots, pausing every now and then to belch loudly in the direction of the trees.

"This is ridiculous," Ellanden hissed. "We should set the beast on fire and be done."

Evie flashed him a hard look.

"If we gave credence to everyone who said that about you—there wouldn't be a piece big enough left to bury. And for the record, I've been *trying* to set it on fire. I can't."

"Why the hell not—"

"I don't know," she interrupted fiercely. "Maybe it has something to do with my massive cranial trauma, you little worm!"

The argument paused as the ogre uprooted a small tree.

"Perfect." Ellanden let out a tired laugh. "Now it's a fair fight."

Delighted by its own ingenuity, the beast swung the tree back and forth like a child who'd stolen his father's sword, taking out half the garden fence in the process. A violent gust of wind hit the side of the shed, and the unlucky trio braced themselves on the other side.

Evie revisited the idea of fleeing in terror, while Asher glanced at the fae in concern.

"Are you up for this?"

It had all the key ingredients to make the prince's perfect day. A ferocious monster, a thrill of adrenaline, the weight of a prophecy, and staggering odds. Combine all that with the fact that the beast had armed itself with a small redwood, and the prince couldn't have designed it better himself.

But that delightful sense of masochism wasn't enough to sew his flesh back together. It was the second time in as many weeks that the fae had been stabbed in the chest. On top of an invasion and a shipwreck. Those wounds were piling up, coming too swiftly on the heels of one another.

Regardless, he took one look at the bloodthirsty ogre and flashed a winning smile.

"Always."

"He's not," Evie said at the same time, slipping into an unintentional impression of the fae's mother. "You're not. You got *stabbed*, Ellanden."

She made it sound embarrassing. Like he'd slipped getting out of bed.

"This morning," he protested. "It's well past the afternoon."

They watched as the beast tore down another sapling.

"There's a giant hole where your heart's supposed to be."

He gave the fire-poker a quick spin.

"You've been saying that for years."

There was a chance they might have fallen into old habits and simply turned on each other, but the vampire interceded with his usual threat.

"Be quiet or I'll bite you."

They obeyed with matching sulks, turning their attention back to the garden. Asher glanced between them, weighing the options in his mind.

By his estimation, the solution was simple. He would kick out the back wall and spirit each of them to safety before dealing with the beast himself. But such logic had never played well with the others. Were he even to suggest such a thing, they were likely to turn on him instead.

"Look at him," Ellanden teased, without ever taking his eyes off the garden. "Right now he's debating which of us he'd going to grab first."

Evie smiled humorlessly, watching the monster slowly advance. "Not if he wants to be single."

The vampire sighed, recalculating on the fly. Despite suffering a massive concussion, his girlfriend appeared to be steady enough. The fae was a different story.

"Truth," he said quietly, stepping into Ellanden's line of sight. "Can you do this? I don't know what happened back in the forest, but you're no good to anyone dead."

"Not much good to anyone alive, either," Evie whispered helpfully.

"I'm fine," Ellanden insisted as the vampire lifted the arm holding the fire-poker, rotating it slowly and checking for breaks. "Stop your mothering. We have bigger problems outside."

Problems that were getting closer by the second.

"You know," Evie said authoritatively, "this is *exactly* the suicidal bullcrap we were just—"

"—just acknowledging that we all secretly felt the same," the fae interrupted harshly. "That's right, you obnoxious little dreamer. So I believe the correct response is to back the hell off." He yanked his arm free. "Ash, I love you—but I'm about to punch you in the face."

Whether or not he would have made good on the threat, the rest of them would never know. Because in that exact moment, the entire shed flew into the air.

The friends froze where they stood, trying to process how they were suddenly outside. Then a giant shadow loomed over them and they lifted their heads slowly to stare up at the beast.

For a split second, words failed them. Then Evie glanced swiftly at the others.

"Should we...you know...charge?"

THERE WAS A MIGHTY roar as the ogre threw up both meaty arms, preparing to crush the trio where they stood. But when they smashed back to the earth, the friends were no longer there.

Granted, they hadn't gotten very far.

Seven hells!

Evie's knees buckled at the impact, sending her sprawling headfirst into the cabbages.

The idea to charge had been instantly abandoned, as had the idea to stand their ground. In the absence of any long-distance weapons, the best way to fight such a creature would be to attack from all sides—hoping to disorient it to the point of being unable to properly attack in return.

The idea was to keep their distance. And keep moving at all times.

Of course, they hadn't factored in the creature's ungodly size.

A pair of profanities rang from the opposite sides of the garden as the creature whirled around in a circle, sending the boys flying with each thundering step. Asher had managed to get to his feet, only to be instantly knocked down again. Ellanden was clinging to a nearby fence-post, glaring in a helpless sort of way while clutching weakly at his chest.

Even from the other side of the property, the princess saw the crimson stain as the fae's new bandages soaked through with blood. The ogre must have seen it, too, because the instant the blood scented the air it launched itself in his direction with a truly deafening cry.

"Ellanden!" she screamed, scrambling off the ground.

A glint of silver caught her eye and she looked down to see a tiny dagger in the grass. The same one the fae had lent her to go hunting—it must have flown right out of her hand.

She picked it up without a second thought and hurled it straight at the ogre, burying the blade in the back of its neck. It was a strike that would have been death to any other creature, but in this case the blade wasn't long enough to hit anything of value. The beast simply paused, scratched curiously at the back of its head, then continued tearing at a deadly speed right towards the fae.

Fortunately, she wasn't the only one coming to the prince's defense.

There was a streak of shadow, so fast the princess might have imagined it, as Asher flew across the garden and leapt straight onto the creature's back. The ogre screeched to a stop, letting out a wild cry and trying to shake him loose. Its massive hands clawed blindly at its back, but the vampire was far too skilled for that. He dodged each one swiftly, anchoring his feet against its putrid skin before yanking out the princess' knife and stabbing it again and again into the beast's head.

This time, the blade seemed to register.

With an ear-splitting howl the ogre abandoned its prize and stumbled painfully across the yard, swaying to and fro as it tried to maintain its balance. The sound was incredible. Both the fae and the princess clapped reflexive hands over their ears. The vampire would most certainly have done the same, but he was clinging with grim determination to the blade.

In what looked like slow motion he yanked it free and buried it into the creature's skin, driving it deeper with all his might. Thick drops of blood rained over the lawn. There was a precarious moment where it looked as though the ogre was about to fall.

Then it stumbled inside the cottage...taking the vampire along with it.

Both Evie and Ellanden froze in horror, staring towards the house, listening to the distant crashes, waiting for at least one of them to emerge. One second crawled after the next, each taking a faltering step forward, then a familiar voice echoed across the lawn.

"Run!" Asher shouted from somewhere inside. "Get to the—"

There was a sudden cry, then everything went quiet.

NO!

The next few seconds were just a blur. With matching shouts the princess and the fae threw themselves forward, streaking like lightning across the shadowy lawn. They didn't think twice about their own injuries. They didn't think twice about the giant monster waiting on the other side. They reached the cottage at the same time and burst through the door...only to freeze once again.

...*Asher?*

The vampire was slumped against the far side of the room, a veil of bloody hair draped over his eyes. Both legs were splayed out at an odd angle, a far cry from his usual grace, and judging by the suspicious trail of blood painted down the cabinets it seemed as though the monster had hurled him full-strength at the ceiling before getting distracted by the embers of the dying fire.

"Asher?"

The word choked out of the princess, lodging somewhere in her throat. It didn't seem possible that it carried all the way across the room, but somehow it must have, because a second later the vampire blinked opened his eyes. He couldn't see past the thick legs of the ogre, still trampling around in between, but his head lifted ever so slightly, angled towards the door.

"I'll get him," Evie breathed. "You take that."

If she'd proposed such a thing just a few minutes earlier, Ellanden would have slapped her across the face. But the fae's dark eyes were already locked on the creature, burning with a very particular kind of hate. He nodded ever so slightly, then the two of them split in opposite directions.

One leapt with a wild cry on top of the ogre.

The other slid between its legs to the other side of the room.

"Ash," Evie panted, lifting his head carefully off the floor. A stream of blood seeped between her fingers as she cradled him in her lap. "Asher, wake up. We need to leave."

The vampire's eyes fluttered open again before locking with sudden focus upon her face. A silent look passed between them—one that transcended the nuisance of words. Then his hand drifted to the back of his head with an adorably adolescent, "...ow."

She laughed in spite of herself, stray tears sliding down her face. On the other side of the room the prince was doing all he could to distract the ogre, attacking with the fury of a nova. But a small barricade of debris had fallen in front of the door, and they were running out of time.

"If I lift you to your feet, think you can make it to those stairs?"

Asher gazed at her a moment longer, his lips curving with a lovely smile.

"Of course."

Her eyebrows shot into her hairline.

"Of course?"

He smiled again, looking quite content to lie there staring.

"You're so beautiful, Everly. I should tell you all the time."

Crap.

"To your credit, you *do* tell me all the time." She heaved him upwards, keeping one arm looped around her neck for balance. "And that's a mighty fine concussion you've got."

His eyes twinkled like she'd made a joke.

"Just like yours!" For a moment, he looked truly delighted. Then his face clouded with sudden concern. "Evie...we should be more careful."

She opened her mouth to answer, then patted him on the back with a smile. "Yes, we should."

A sudden voice echoed across the room.

"Are you two finished chatting?" Ellanden shouted, driving the ogre back with nothing more than a rusted candlestick. "Because I could use a little help over here!"

"We've given up!" Asher called cheerfully. "We're retreating to higher ground!"

The fae cast a quick look over his shoulder then smashed his boot into the hearth, sending up a swirling cloud of sparks. While the beast looked on in wonder the three friends darted up the stairs, dragging the vampire between them, scaling the house one level at a time.

When they finally got to the attic, they came to a sudden stop—shutting the door behind them before falling in a breathless heap upon the floor.

"I want to thank you," Ellanden panted. "For volunteering us for this."

The fae was looking decidedly worse for wear after his skirmish with the ogre. In addition to having torn completely through his bandages, there were bits of carrot and candlewax in his hair.

It was *almost* enough to make the princess feel sorry for him.

"Would you rather my grandmother have done it?" she demanded.

He shot her a cold look. "Your grandmother...who can shoot fire?"

She ignored this, turning to Asher.

They were safe for the moment, but there was no telling when the ogre might come crashing up the stairs. There was also no telling whether the structural integrity of the stairs could possibly support said ogre, meaning whatever was going to happen had better happen fast.

"Honey—talk to me. How are you feeling?"

He looked a little steadier. His eyes were focused and he was no longer leaning on her for support. That being said, the pain had caught up and his lovely face was a frightful shade of white.

He ground his teeth together, trying to be brave.

"I'm fine. What's the plan?"

You're lying. I'd know it even without the bond.

"Is it your head?" she asked quickly, kneeling up beside him for a better look. "There was an awful lot of bleeding..."

"It's my hand." He pushed her gently back, keeping her at arm's length. "And it's fine. We can deal with everything when we get back—"

"Your hand?" she interrupted, rolling up his sleeve. "What happened to your...?"

She trailed off a moment later.

"...oh."

There was a reason the fae was giving her so much grief for being unable to summon those magical flames. Few things out there could do more damage than dragon fire.

My psychotic family strikes again.

"Okay...yikes." She offered him an apologetic stare. "On behalf of my grandmother, let me be the first to say...that was a *total* accident."

Ellanden peeled away the bloody fabric, seeing it for himself.

"Asher, that is *disgusting*," he said disapprovingly.

"I think it makes you look dashing," Evie countered swiftly, feeling the sudden need to save face. "Really brings out that spark of adventure in your eyes."

"Could you both stop channeling your fathers and *help* me?" Asher interjected, pushing to his feet in exasperation. "I am *bleeding* here."

Evie's face tightened with concern, while Ellanden gestured to his chest.

"So am I."

The vampire's eyes narrowed with a glare.

"Yes, but that's hardly a rare thing for you. You know, I think Evie was right. We need to put you on some kind of..." He trailed off, staring at the princess in shock. "What are you doing?"

She knelt in front of him, offering out her wrist.

"What do you mean? You asked for help."

Ellanden's eyes shot between them, growing wider with every pass.

"I wanted you to get me a bandage," Asher spluttered, still out of sorts, "or at least try to curtail your terrible jokes—"

"I'm not ripping my dress, and the jokes are out of the question," she replied briskly, rolling up her sleeve. "You won't heal otherwise—the burn is too deep. And that's not even mentioning whatever damage that thing downstairs did to your head. So here—take it."

When he hesitated again, she flashed an impish smile.

"It's nothing you haven't done before..."

His eyes warmed at the memory, smiling in spite of himself. There had been several times the previous evening when the vampire's fangs had gotten away from him.

Both he and the princess had enjoyed each occasion very much.

"All right," he said softly, taking her wrist, "thanks."

The fae leapt to his feet in alarm. "Seriously?! Right in front of me?!"

"You saw him do it once before—that day by the lake." Evie shot the vampire a self-important look, as if there was a chance he'd forgotten. "When I *saved* your *life*."

He flashed a quick grin, poised an inch above her skin.

"Yeah, gorgeous. I remember."

"That was different," Ellanden said stiffly, watching with morbid fascination in spite of his best efforts to turn away. "He was missing giant pieces of his neck, just a breath away from death itself. Asher, either injure yourself more seriously or stop complaining—"

The vampire lifted the princess' wrist, and the fae smacked it down again.

"I'm serious!" he insisted. "It's different now that you share a bond! What am I supposed to do when the two of you start tearing each other's clothes off?"

Evie shrugged. "...be jealous?"

"Watch for the ogre," Asher replied sweetly, tugging her closer. "You like that kind of stuff right, Ellanden? Fighting beasts? *Provoking* them? How about you focus on doing that...so I can have a little moment with my girlfriend."

Before the fae could answer, his fangs pierced her skin.

Evie's eyes snapped shut as she leaned forward, wrapping her other arm involuntarily around his neck. No matter how many times they shared blood, she didn't think she would ever get over it.

The rush of sensation. That pull deep in her stomach. The overwhelming need to get closer, no matter what the situation, no matter what the cost—

"Okay...I think that's quite enough."

An awkward hand eased her backwards and she opened her eyes to discover that she was straddling Asher's lap. His eyes shot open as well, looking just as surprised to see her there. The same way he was surprised to find his free hand sliding up the princess' back.

They scrambled away from each other as the fae stared deliberately at the wall.

"Worst. Day. Ever."

"Sorry about that," Asher flushed, pushing swiftly to his feet. With the princess' blood flying fresh through his system, there wasn't a single mark or injury on his skin. Even the burns on his hand had vanished, leaving nothing but smooth skin in their wake. "I'll just head back down and—"

But there was no need to return to the ogre. In the midst of their blood-trade, the ogre had found them. And it looked particularly delighted to have done so.

"Crap!"

A massive hand burst into the room, tearing the door right off the wall. It crashed down the stairs in an explosion of splinters, to reveal an unspeakably grotesque smile.

"THERE YOU ARE!"

"Seven hells," Evie breathed, feeling suddenly faint. "It can talk."

In hindsight, it wasn't the best time to have lost a large amount of blood. The second she pushed to her feet, she started swaying for balance. (Granted, that might have been the ogre.) There was a distorted ringing in her head as her friends started shouting. (Granted, that might have been the ogre, too.) It wasn't until she lifted her hands that she even realized what she was about to do.

"That's enough, Clancy."

A wave of dragon fire, surpassing even the famed Adelaide Grey, poured out of her palms, consuming the beast in a writhing ball of teeth and screams. Her friends let out a shout and leapt backwards as she took an instinctive step forward, curving her hands and tilting her head as the fire circled round and round the monster's head. It made a final grab for them, showering the room in a spray of boiling blood before falling with a tremendous howl back to the ground.

Inconvenient even in death…it took the stairs right along with it.

"That's it for me," Evie panted in exhaustion, oblivious to the sudden precariousness of their situation. "Time for a nap."

The men shot each other a quick look, each too shell-shocked to move. Then Asher grabbed the princess and Ellanden took a tentative step forward, peering down into the fiery abyss.

They were trapped in the attic with no exit strategy. Not only that, but the house below was caving in and that deadly fire was creeping up the walls. A dozen painted faces stared up at them, melting with judgmental stares as a column of smoke spiraled up into the room.

The smoke broke through the fatigue and Evie let out a strangled gasp.

"Seven hells!" She coughed violently, clinging to the vampire's arms. "I'm so sorry, I didn't mean to—"

"None of that," Asher said quickly. "You saved us."

The fae nodded in silence, but his face was strained.

There was simply no way to get down. The house had dissolved into a fiery inferno. At any second, those final support beams would give out and they'd be sucked in as well.

"What are we going to do?" Evie gasped again. "You guys—what are we going to do!"

The fae glanced down a second longer, then looked up with the hint of a smile.

"As much as I'd hate to play into the stereotype...we could always jump out the window."

A charged silence fell over the room.

Then Asher bowed his head with a sigh.

"At this point, I'm likely to be charged," he muttered as they raced across the room and broke open the glass, peering down at the garden. "Some kind of criminal negligence. Leaving a lunatic to his own devices, enabling a psychopath...that sort of thing."

Ellanden clapped him on the shoulder with a breathless grin. "I'm excited, too!"

The vampire shook his head with a reluctant smile as the house groaned beneath them. The supports were failing. The entire thing tilted as they stepped together onto the ledge.

"You ready?" he whispered to Evie.

She threw him a quick look before staring at the now-moonlit forest. Somewhere just a few miles away, her grandmother was waiting in those trees. Her friends were waiting a bit farther than that.

"Always."

Then, for what felt like the hundredth time, the friends grabbed each other's hands and leapt into the open air...

Chapter 6

It was a dramatic leap...and a crippling fall.

The friends crashed to the ground with little else to slow their momentum than the broken vegetables strewn across the garden. Each one let out a muffled curse the second they struck the dirt then lay depressingly still, secretly wishing they'd taken their chances with the fire.

"Honey?"

The princess heard Asher before she saw him, crawling across a bed of parsnips to get to her side. A pair of cool hands slipped under her ribcage, lifting her gently off the ground.

"Are you okay?" he breathed, smoothing back her tangled hair to make a worried study of her face. "Anything broken? Do you want to shift—"

"I'm fine." She discreetly flexed each of her limbs, wondering if it was remotely true. Her eyes made a quick sweep of the garden. "Where's Ellanden?"

"I'm here."

An arm waved weakly in the air before falling back to the dirt.

In a bizarre reversal of roles, the princess had managed to survive the fall with at least a modicum of dignity. While the fae had landed in a thick stretch of mud.

She stared in morbid fascination, searching for his face.

"Can he breathe like that?"

There was a faint stirring, follow by a muffled voice.

"...not really."

The vampire leaned back in relief, making a valiant effort to keep a grin off his face.

"I thought you were going to do some aerial flips or something," he called. "Swing from the rafters and still manage to land on your feet."

The fae lifted his head slowly from the mud. "Yeah...so did I."

———

EVEN ONCE THEY'D MANAGED to extract themselves from the garden, things weren't looking much better. The princess was secretly spinning, either from the five-story drop or the blood loss, and the fae had reached the point where he was no longer able to stand on his own.

"This is ridiculous," he muttered, limping slowly down the path with an arm thrown reluctantly around Asher's neck. "I can do it myself—you don't need to help me."

The vampire nodded patiently, just as he'd done since they'd left the cottage.

"I know. Just humor me for a while, all right?"

For the last few minutes they'd been walking at a painful speed through the forest, sticking to the road whenever possible as they made their way through the moonlit trees. They had no real way to find Adelaide, short of stumbling upon her, but the princess could already smell the scorched grass where she'd burned the side of the mountain, and the fortress wasn't too far away from that.

To be honest, if it wasn't for the catastrophic injuries two of them had sustained it might have been a rather peaceful walk. There weren't any people in this stretch of the woods, nothing to break the silence but the occasional call of nightingales as they drifted through the violet sky.

Of course, they'd been blessed with an ongoing commentary.

"I'm the invincible one, remember?" Ellanden flashed the vampire a look, only half-joking, as they stumbled up the side of a ravine. "I'm the brave one—who generally saves all the others?"

Asher laughed under his breath, lifting him the rest of the way. "Yeah, Landi. You're the brave one."

The fae nodded stiffly, fighting the perpetual need to scream.

"Good," he panted, raising a hand to his chest. "Because I've had a stretch of bad luck here, and I'd hate for you to get the wrong—"

His eyes snapped shut with a grimace and he paused suddenly on the side of the road. Asher paused with him, a gentle hand resting on his back.

It had been that way since they left.

Whenever the fae was watching, the vampire stood passively by his side. Whenever he wasn't, those dark eyes shone with the same wild concern dilating them now.

They swept quickly over him, memorizing every break and bruise.

"I wish I could give you my blood," he murmured softly.

Ellanden's eyes snapped open in surprise. "What?"

The vampire flushed and looked away. "Nothing, I just—"

But the fae started laughing. Ironically enough, it distracted him from the pain long enough to keep moving—detaching himself from Asher as he limped slowly up the road.

"If there's one thing that could make this day worse," he chuckled, bracing a constant hand against his chest, "it's me drinking your blood."

The vampire stared after him in shock, then started smiling himself. He was still standing there when Evie walked up behind him, slipping her hand into his own.

"So that was a nonstarter—with the blood-letting?"

He chuckled quietly, lacing their fingers together. "I guess so."

They continued walking for a while, wandering along several paces behind the fae, when he spoke up again suddenly, trusting his friend would be too distracted to overhear.

"It shouldn't be a nonstarter," he said abruptly, eyes fixed on the road. "It isn't a crazy idea that the two of us would bond...especially not after what happened this morning."

The princess was so surprised, she actually pulled him to a stop.

"Are you serious?"

Since they were just children, the inseparable trio had debated the prospect of sealing their fellowship with an everlasting bond. Raised on the legacy of their parents, it was impossible not to consider such things. But there was never anyone arguing for the other side.

Blood bonds were charming in theory and terrifying in real life. Even for three adventurous young immortals, the idea of an eternal covenant was something better left to the adults. Never had they actually considered such a thing. And yet...two of them had already sealed their fate.

"They did it on the eve of battle," she continued when Asher didn't say anything. "They did it because their prophecy specifically said, *united by marriage, united by blood*. They didn't have any other choice—"

"Some of them did," he interrupted softly, eyes on the back of Ellanden's head. "And it kept all of them safer once it was done. I'm not saying we should actually do it, I'm just..." He trailed off with a sigh, quickening his pace. "I'm not saying anything at all."

The princess matched his stride, stealing secret looks from the corner of her eye.

He didn't press the matter further and they were both quick to let the subject drop, but there was something oddly practiced about his words—like it wasn't the first time he'd considered saying them. It was paired with a look that made her wonder how many times he'd thought of such a thing before. She'd seen traces of it back at the vampire camp, when Diana had mentioned it herself.

"It's a wonder you haven't bonded with them. That's what your father did. Then you'd never have to worry, then you could know they were safe."

"What about you?"

She lifted her head suddenly, to see him staring back at her. When her face blanked in confusion, he softened with an affectionate smile.

"How are you feeling?" he prompted, giving her hand a little squeeze. "I felt terrible taking any blood, when you were sporting injuries of your own. If it had been anything less than dragon fire...and you must be hungry," he added suddenly. "You haven't eaten anything since last night."

She let out a sudden laugh, resting her head against his arm.

"I know you don't believe in 'twinning', but you sound like a whole different person after drinking my blood. Am I really that much a stream-of-consciousness?"

"No," the vampire answered charitably.

"Yes," the fae chimed in at the same time.

She laughed again, marveling at how strange their conversations had become.

"So what shall we get you for dinner?" Asher pressed, leaning down without thinking to kiss the top of her head. "Would you like some venison? Rabbit stew? There will be time enough for me to hunt once we get back—"

"Is this going to become a thing?" she interrupted playfully. "Just because we're together-*together*, you're suddenly concerned with whether I'm getting enough food?"

He startled in surprise, possibly at her hinted use of the phrase 'together', but it was replaced with an easy smile. "Maybe...but you didn't answer my question."

"I'd like some whiskey," Ellanden volunteered, slowing down until the pair of them caught up. "As long as you're taking dinner orders, perhaps you could run to the store room and—"

"*Everly!*"

The trio paused in the middle of the road, watching as a breathless woman sprinted towards them. She didn't stop or slow her pace, until her granddaughter was safe in her arms.

"I saw the smoke!" she gasped, clutching Evie impossibly tighter. "I was just..." She trailed off, staring at their soot-covered faces. "So it's really over? The house...it's gone?"

It was hard to say which answer she wanted to hear. Chances were, the queen wasn't certain herself. In the end, the most they could do was tell the truth.

"It's gone," Evie repeated softly, giving her a final squeeze. "Everything...it's all over."

The woman stared at her for a moment, then her face warmed into a radiant smile.

"Time to move forward, then."

The princess linked their arms together, setting off once more down the trail.

"Time to move forward."

CONSIDERING EACH OF the three friends recently had swan-dived from the top of a burning building, they were in surprisingly high spirits by the time they crossed the woods. The prospect of sleep and a warm meal had brightened them considerably, and as the sounds of the fortress drifted through the last of the trees the only one who looked remotely apprehensive was the queen.

"So your friend, Seth," she repeated with a hint of trepidation, trying to keep the story straight, "he's a shifter? And after the slavers were defeated, you relocated his pack into the fort?"

Evie gave her a sympathetic squeeze.

It was sometimes easy to forget that the last time the queen had wandered freely around the realm, all magic had been strictly forbidden. Slavers had been granted royal protection, and if anyone was found to be a shifter they'd have been dragged back to the castle and hanged.

"You're going to love him," the princess reassured her. "All of them. And there really aren't all that many. The fort sleeps several hundred, but it's not even half-full."

The queen flinched involuntarily, and the boys shot her a punishing look.

It was also easy to forget that it was the first time in fifty years Adelaide had seen another human face besides her deceased husband and her psychotic son.

"Most of them will be asleep," Asher lied smoothly. "We'll just slip inside and find you a room. Any introductions you wish can be made in the morning."

The queen smiled weakly. "You're sweet. Who knew vampires could be sweet?"

"They aren't," Ellanden replied brightly. "See—*that's* something that hasn't changed."

"He's right," Evie said authoritatively, ignoring the look on her boyfriend's face. "You have nothing to worry about. Except that people don't really use the common tongue. We communicate now in a series of percussive clicks and exaggerated sighs."

The queen gave her a long look before shaking her head.

"You're most certainly Katy's daughter..."

PERHAPS THE CRIES OF the ogre had echoed through the forest, or perhaps those inside the fortress had merely seen the smoke. Either way, there was a mild explosion moment the friends crossed the drawbridge and stepped through the gate.

"Ellanden!"

The fae lifted his head as a door burst open on the second story and a breathless young witch raced outside. There were people her path, but she didn't stop for them. When too many paused on the crowded stairway, she merely leapt over the side.

Her face was pale and her lovely eyes were brimming with tears as she sprinted straight towards him, waves of moonlit hair flying out behind.

"We thought you were dead!" she gasped, racing across the cobblestones. "We thought—"

She didn't slow down when she reached him. She didn't stop to think. She stretched onto the tips of her toes, grabbed both sides of his face...and kissed him right on the mouth.

Seven hells!

Ellanden froze in astonishment, a lovely statue under her hands.

There was a moment when he leaned into it. A perfect, fleeting moment when his eyes closed, his fingers touched her face, and he looked as truly happy as the princess had ever seen.

That moment shattered into a million pieces as he forced himself back.

"I...I can't..."

It was barely a whisper, but the witch heard it loud and clear. Her face paled in silent horror before she turned on her heel and ran straight back the way she'd come.

He stared after her, looking like someone had stabbed him in the heart.

"Freya!" he called desperately. "Freya, I'm sorry—"

There was a commotion above them as another young woman tore down the stairwell, looking almost as manic as the first. The princess' head was still spinning, but in that moment she realized there was a very important part of the queen's story she had accidentally left out.

"Oh shit," Asher murmured, remembering at the same time. He flashed another look at Ellanden before taking a step back as Cosette screeched to a stop in front of them.

"What the hell happened!" she demanded. "Where have you been! We saw smoke from the top of the bell tower. I was about to head after you, when Seth said I should wait."

The shifter emerged on the balcony above her, sporting a fresh black eye.

"Those eyes," Adelaide gasped, lifting a hand slowly to her chest. "I would know those eyes anywhere..."

Only then did the fae princess seem to notice there was someone else in their group. She stared at the queen a suspended moment before her mouth fell open in shock.

"I must be dreaming."

Evie nudged them together with a little smile.

"Adelaide Grey...meet Cosette Damaris. Your granddaughter."

The queen took a step forward, wanting nothing more than to gather the child in her arms. But Cosette was completely frozen—those dark eyes widening to saucers in her exquisite face. In a flash Adelaide adjusted her strategy, clasping her hands together with a warm smile.

"It's a long story. Perhaps we should tell it inside..."

THE NEXT FEW HOURS were spent in deep discussion as the three friends recounted everything that had happened since they set off into the woods. From their surprise run-in with the slavers, to their rescue by the queen, right down to their battle with the ogre in the middle of a vegetable patch.

It wasn't the easiest conversation. Particularly when they got to the news about Kaleb Grey.

"So if he's your son...you and Rhys..." Cosette's eyes widened as she made the connection for the first time. "That would make him...my uncle?"

"Half-uncle," Evie corrected, catching the look on her grandmother's face. "Not that those distinctions are important..."

Seth leaned forward, arms resting on his knees.

"And he's the one in the prophecy?" He glanced a bit nervously at the queen before shaking his head. "I don't understand...why would he want the stone?"

"He wants the power to take over the five kingdoms," Adelaide answered softly. "The stone is merely the first step."

"But you said it has a dark influence—"

"Power is power." She bowed her head with a sigh. "Kaleb doesn't care where it comes from, as long as he can use it to achieve his own ends." She glanced at the princess. "If your mother was able to use one stone to unite the realm, it stands to reason he could do the same with its twin."

This is why we shouldn't collect rocks. This is why we shouldn't have libraries.

Seth nodded slowly, glancing around the room. "So...this doesn't change anything? We're still going to destroy the stone?"

Evie leaned against the window, staring up at the moon.

Yes, they were still going to destroy the stone. If they could find it. And if they could find it first. But as for the rest...she was afraid it changed everything.

THE GATHERING ENDED on a rather subdued note.

Cosette had sat beside the queen the entire time, though she was too shy to actually speak to the woman. Seth had been furious that the others had fought the ogre on their own, but he looked personally touched that they'd stopped it from going to the fort where his little sisters were sleeping.

...and Freya wasn't there.

"I don't understand," Evie said to Asher as the two of them wandered along the corridor. "I don't understand why Ellanden didn't go after her. I don't understand why he isn't going after her *right now*. You can tell he wants to. What the heck is stopping him?"

Asher shrugged with a thoughtful frown. "Maybe he doesn't want to."

She turned to face him. "Did you see the look on his face when they kissed?"

He chuckled quietly, beams of torchlight flickering across his face. "I stopped trying long ago to unravel the fae's twisted mind. Besides," he pulled her abruptly closer, looking down with a grin, "I haven't had a moment alone with you since last night. I'd much rather do this..."

The kiss took her breath away, stealing the witty comebacks right off her lips. Even though she saw it coming, even though he'd done it a hundred times before, there was no way to prepare.

She didn't think she'd ever be prepared. There was no preparing oneself for a kiss like that.

She could only close her eyes and let it happen. And pray for a hundred more.

"I wanted to do that from the moment I woke up," he whispered, pulling back a few inches to see her face. "When you weren't there...I thought I'd go crazy with waiting."

A blush warmed her cheeks as she stretched up and kissed him again.

"You didn't guess I was stranded in the woods after setting the mountain on fire?"

He laughed quietly, running his thumbs along her cheeks. "I should have. I'm off my game." His eyes twinkled with mischief. "Ever since last night, I've been completely distracted."

She pulled back with a serious expression. "What happened last night?"

There was a pause.

"You're a terrible person."

"I'm serious," she insisted. "Did you have a funny dream?"

He cocked his head, trying to hold back a smile. "If you've actually forgotten, I'd be happy to remind you."

"Oh yeah?" She wrapped her arms around his neck with a grin. "Well, if you *insist*, I suppose I could be persuaded..."

The sound of footsteps echoed across the courtyard and she pulled back to see Adelaide walking along the corridor on the other side, pausing uncertainly as she tried to find her room.

Evie stared in silence, feeling abruptly protective before glancing up at her boyfriend. "Actually, do you mind if—"

"Go," he interrupted with a smile. "I'll wait up for you."

She gave him another quick kiss, then flew down the stairwell—darting across the courtyard and climbing the stairs on the other side. By the time she got there the queen had already found her chambers, but she looked up with a smile as her granddaughter froze awkwardly in the frame.

"Everly! I thought you'd turned in for the night."

The princess flushed and tucked back her hair.

"It's Evie, actually...and I just wanted to make sure you had everything you needed."

Adelaide glanced around the sparse room—soldiers' barracks, repurposed by whatever slaver had happened to spend the night. Nothing but a bed, a dresser, and a tiny mirror. But still, the queen beamed like it was some kind of miracle.

"I have more than enough," she answered warmly, beckoning the girl inside. "But it was sweet of you to check on me. I'm not used to...well, I haven't spoken to anyone new in a long time."

Evie perched tentatively on the edge of the mattress.

"So it was only ever the two of you?" she asked curiously. "For all that time? I mean, until you had Kaleb—"

She caught herself quickly, but Adelaide just shook her head with a smile.

"Yes, it was only me and Rhys. I was told the road near the cottage was common for merchants and travelers, but the enchantment he cast kept even chance encounters at bay."

The princess bowed her head, staring down at her hands.

She couldn't imagine how lonely it must have been. She couldn't imagine how lonely it must still be that very moment. The dirt on the grave was only a few days old.

"...I'm very sorry about Rhys."

The smile remained, though the queen's eyes grew sad.

"I wish you could have known him. I wish you could have known them both," she added suddenly, "before Kaleb changed. Before he turned into the way he is now."

Evie stared at her a moment, then shook her head.

"It's so much to lose," she whispered, feeling suddenly terrible about having burned down the woman's house. "I couldn't imagine...no person should have to lose so much."

A pair of cool fingers tilted up her chin.

"There's a lot that's been gained as well."

A curious silence fell between them, then the queen sat beside her on the bed.

"I don't look at it in terms of loss, Evie. I never have. I lost my children—yes. And that is a pain that still haunts me. But I had Rhys. I had Kaleb—for however long a time." Her eyes lit up as she reached out a tentative hand, curling a lock of the princess' hair. "I have you, my darling. Today, I got to meet not one but *two* granddaughters. That was a greater joy than I could ever have hoped."

She paused suddenly, her eyes filling with happy tears.

"And soon...I'll get to see my children again."

The smile faded slowly from Evie's face.

For longer than she cared to admit, that same thought had sustained her. No matter where she happened to be, no matter what fresh horror lay in store—she would soon see her mother.

In the beginning, it was an unspeakable comfort. Now...she wasn't so sure.

"I should let you sleep," she said softly, pushing to her feet.

With a parting kiss on the cheek, she left her grandmother on the bed and headed back to the courtyard. But she paused at the door—turning back with an impulse she couldn't control.

"You know that she left—my mother." Her voice hardened with a bitter edge. "That crown of hers was holding the realm together...but she gave it up and walked away."

Adelaide stared at her a moment, then bowed her head with a sigh.

"Yes...Kaleb told me." She looked pensively out the window, turning back with a melancholy smile. "Don't judge your mother too harshly, my darling. She thought her only child had been killed. There isn't a way to measure that kind of loss. The most you can do is survive it."

The princess shook her head, gripping hard at the frame. "But she had an obligation—they all did. There were people counting on them. There were entire *kingdoms* counting on them. How could they just—"

"Five years, your mother fought," Adelaide interrupted gently. "Five years, she ripped the world apart looking for you. You would judge her for giving up the crown? I would commend her for getting out of bed."

"But my mother isn't like that," Evie argued. "She's strong. She's the strongest person I—"

"It isn't a matter of strength, sweetheart. It's a matter of grief." She shook her head slowly, trying to explain. "To love something so fiercely, so deeply...to lose one's *child*...you have no idea the unending depths of that pain. It cannot be judged. It cannot be reasoned away. It is well beyond all that. It is something that becomes you, body and soul."

The women bid each other goodnight shortly after and Evie wandered back up the winding corridors, pausing every now and again to gaze up at the light of the moon. It seemed impossible to reconcile, the balance of such unspeakable joy and such devastating sadness. Her grandmother was a perfect blend of the two—a woman who could manage a sincere smile, even with tears in her eyes.

When she spoke of the loss of a child...

Evie shook her head, turning her thoughts deliberately to other things.

There was enough to contend with without venturing into questions of the soul. There was a villain to defeat, a stone to destroy, a prophecy to fulfill. She couldn't afford to lose herself in existentialisms. Someone had to keep their eyes on the horizon. Someone had to keep moving on.

It didn't strike her until much later that she didn't know which grief the queen was talking about. That unending pain from which there was no relief. Which names haunted her in the night?

The twins she lost so long ago...or her youngest son.

Chapter 7

It wasn't until the princess had been wandering for several minutes that she realized she had no idea where she was supposed to go. This was only the second night the friends had spent at the fortress, and she and Asher had spent the first sleeping in a naked tangle beneath the bell tower.

Well...not *quite* sleeping.

A little smile crept up her face as she put the conversation with Adelaide far from her mind and focused on the present instead. On the man waiting for her. On the night they had planned.

As far as she was concerned, she and Asher were at a distinct disadvantage. Yes, they might have an eternity ahead of them, but they'd lost the first sixteen years. There were a lot of wasted moments and missed opportunities, and she intended to start making up for them that very night.

Maybe I could persuade him to take a walk in the forest...away from a fortress full of supernatural ears. We could avoid the part I burned. I could check first for more bear traps—

The sound of quiet voices caught her attention and she came to a pause, gazing across the hallway with a little smile.

It seemed that Asher hadn't known where to go either, so he'd wandered to Ellanden's room instead. The two of them were sitting on either side of the bed, their long legs stretched towards the middle, lost in such deep discussion they hadn't even realized they'd left the door open.

A glass bottle was lying on the blankets between them. Every so often, the fae would lift it to his mouth. Every so often, the vampire would snap sternly and he'd dab some on his chest instead.

"—in the olden days, they tried all sorts of things to get rid of them," the fae was saying, leaning back against the headboard. "Everything from pushing boulders onto their nests, to lacing poison amongst the livestock, right down to flaming catapults to knock them out of the sky."

The princess flitted secretly closer, keeping her back to the wall.

"Flaming catapults?" Asher repeated with a laugh. "They tried using *fire* against a dragon?"

The fae smiled, taking a swig of whiskey. "I'm guessing they learned that lesson pretty quick..."

A chill ran up Evie's shoulders and she froze where she stood.

Dragons. They're talking about how to kill a dragon.

"My father told me once that some fishermen wove these great nets, threw them over the beasts when they glided low over the water. Their wings tangled in the rope and they drowned in the sea." He paused a moment before adding, "Of course, most of the ships sank in the process."

Asher laughed again, trailing his fingers absentmindedly in the flame of a candle. After a few seconds, his dark eyes grew thoughtful as the smile faded from his face.

"Catapults and poison...it would be a lot easier to fight him as a man."

Evie's breath caught in her chest.

Kaleb.

"Not a man," Ellanden corrected wryly. "A sorcerer. And to be honest, I'd rather take my chances with the dragon. At least then you know what's coming. A magical legacy passed from one wizard to the next? There's no telling what tricks he might have up his sleeve."

Unseen by the others, the princess leaned back against the wall—lifting her eyes once more to the moon while her heart pounded away in her chest.

When Seth had asked if their plans had changed, she'd taken cover in the logistics. They still had to find the stone. They still had to destroy it. They still had to drive that invasive darkness out of the realm and restore things to the way they had been before.

It was easy to think of it that way, in simple terms of black and white.

It got a lot harder when that darkness had a name.

It got harder still when the same blood ran between them.

"—told you to disinfect it," Asher was saying. "The last thing we need is you developing a fever the second we set out on the road."

There was a swish of whiskey, followed by a hiss of pain.

"I've done it already, Ash. The wound is clean—"

The princess took a deep breath and stepped through the doorway.

"Well if it isn't my two favorite men," she said with a forced smile. "Lying around as usual, bunch of lazy degenerates..."

They glanced up with matching smiles. Ellanden offered her the bottle.

"How did it go with Adelaide?" Asher asked, making a quick study of her face. He couldn't tell if the smile was real. But it was the end of a very long day. Perhaps she was simply tired.

"It went fine." She took a long drink of whiskey before gesturing to a pile of fabric on the bed. "I see you found a shirt."

The fae nodded with a faint smile.

"Not that Asher's letting me wear it—the man has anointed himself healer. *Again*."

She settled down between them, draping her legs over their own.

"Perhaps he simply likes the sight of you like this. So vulnerable, so exposed."

"I thought of that," Ellanden murmured, eyeing the vampire suspiciously whilst taking the bottle back for himself. "And you wanted us to *bond*. How would you keep your hands off me?"

Asher closed his eyes with eternal patience. "It would take all my restraint."

The princess grinned in spite of herself, taking another swig of whiskey.

Despite the troubles plaguing them, despite her newfound family and the fresh hell they were bringing to their door, it was impossible not to take comfort in the familiarity of the scene.

It didn't matter where they were—in a castle, in the woods, even in the dark enchantment of a sorcerer's cave—all her life...it had always been the three of them.

How many times had they sat like this? Legs draped over legs, hair falling into eyes, passing a bottle in between. How many times had they talked by the light of a slow-burning candle, sharing secret fears and even more secret dreams as the night slowly surrendered itself into dawn?

Of course, she had plans to change all that. A conversation had just started up again, the men had just relaxed back into their usual rhythm, when she hit them both with the sudden—

"So what were you talking about?"

They tensed imperceptibly beneath her, flashing each other a secret look.

"Fishing," Asher answered automatically.

"Yeah, fishing." Ellanden made a nonsensical gesture with his hands. "The, uh...the nets."

She nodded slowly, fighting back a smile.

If they were being honest, the idea of a vampiric bond was almost superfluous. Yes, it might allow Asher to find them, but as for the compulsive transparency of some eternal union?

We're already there.

"Fishing. Wow. After the day we had?"

At this point, Asher bowed his head with a blush. But Ellanden dug in hard.

"I've always been obsessed with fishing," he said stiffly. "Fishing and tales of death." His face lightened suddenly as the charade fell away. "Actually, I was thinking of hunting tomorrow, try to restock the pack's food supply. That plan fell apart this morning. We could stop by the river, do some fishing on the way. I also need to find my new bow."

Asher held back his initial censure and flashed him a quizzical look. "Your bow?"

This time it was the fae's turn to flush.

"The one the village gave me," he said softly. "I lost it in the woods, when...you know."

For all his high standards, for all his royal finery, the fae had grown impossibly attached to the savage little creation. He couldn't bear the thought of being without it.

Evie leaned forward sympathetically, clapping him on the back. "When you got caught in a *giant bear trap*?"

She had been practicing the phrase, reveling in the frightful absurdity. She'd done the same with similarly dreadful things. *Basilisks, giants, embroidery*. Each dark and terrible in its own right.

Ellanden's eyes cooled and he took the whiskey for himself.

"We may need to amend that story for posterity," he murmured, swishing it contemplatively in the bottle. "Maybe we could say it was a hellhound...or some kind of demon boar."

Asher grinned in spite of himself.

"Landi, we just fought an ogre. You really need to make up some—"

"The ogre—that's perfect!" the fae cried. "We'll say it was the ogre!" He drained the rest of the bottle, feeling abruptly pleased with how the day had turned out. "*That's* a fantastic story. You know, I wonder if we could even—"

A scream echoed from downstairs.

"Help me!"

The friends froze on the bed, staring at each other in alarm.

"Somebody help!"

They were on their feet the next moment, tearing down the stairs to join the large crowd already gathered in the courtyard. With a sense of dread they elbowed their way closer, only to be faced with a terrifying sight. Charlotte was weeping uncontrollably. Violet was clutched in her arms.

"What's going on?" Evie gasped. "What happened?"

No one noticed her. No one even heard. There was another surge in the crowd as Seth pushed his way forward—much more violently than the friends had done themselves. He froze in terror when his eyes locked on his little sister, her legs swinging lifelessly from their mother's arms.

"Is she..."

Cosette appeared behind him, clutching his hand.

"Mom, is she..." His head jerked once, but he couldn't manage to find the words. He just stood there, white-faced and trembling, speaking in a low, uneven voice. "Tell me she isn't—"

"She's alive," Charlotte cried, seeing him for the first time. "I mean, she's breathing, but something's wrong! Seth, she won't wake—"

"What happened?" Adelaide interrupted, sweeping through the crowd.

Her voice carried an unmistakable note of authority, and for a moment it was exactly what everyone needed. The crowed quieted immediately. Charlotte sucked in a quick breath.

"She was exploring by the tunnels with the other children, when she suddenly collapsed." A pair of tears slipped down her face and she clutched the girl tighter. "There's nothing down there. I wouldn't have let them go otherwise. Just a few empty casks of rum..."

The queen nodded calmly, easing to her side. With a steady hand she took the girl's pulse, leaning closer with a frown as she counted out each silent breath. For a few seconds, no one in the courtyard dared to move. Every pair of panicked eyes was locked on her face.

After what felt like an eternity, she straightened up slowly.

"She's all right," she said softly, her eyes on Charlotte. "But she isn't asleep, her pulse is too faint for that. It almost looks as though she's been drugged."

She paused a moment to let that sink in. Considering the girl had spent her entire young life amongst a fiercely protective pack, it wasn't taken well. An echoing growl filtered through the ranks of those watching. Once it had quieted, she continued on in that same even tone.

"Are you sure there's nothing else by the tunnels?" she pressed. "No one went with her or followed her? No one could have been waiting there?"

Charlotte shook her head, her eyes wide with shock. Both arms had tightened around the child upon hearing the word 'drugged'. Seth strode forward, standing by her side.

"She was playing with the other children," she repeated faintly. "No one else could have been waiting; the tunnel was empty and stops at a dead-end. I went down there myself—"

Seth squeezed her shoulder, clenching his jaw.

"I'll go and check it out," he said quietly, forcing himself to be calm. If there was one thing the Red Hand had given him, it was steady nerves. Still, this was his little sister. His fists were clenched so tight he'd already drawn blood. "If there's anything down there—"

"Please stay," Charlotte whispered, unwilling to part with another of her children when one was still lying helplessly in her arms. "Let someone else check. Seth...*please.*"

His face tightened painfully, as if he was about to refuse. But at that moment Violet stirred weakly, and every thought of the tunnels vanished from his mind.

"That's it, sweetheart." He smoothed back her damp hair, cupping his hands so delicately around that tiny face. "Open your eyes."

Cosette was standing beside him, her face a mask of worry. Freya had pushed her way through the crowd and was standing not far behind, one hand gripping the fae's cloak.

"We'll go," Evie murmured before she'd even considered what she was saying. Her eyes shot to Asher for confirmation and he nodded decisively. "We'll go right now."

It might have been the end of what felt like an endless day, they might have recently limped their way back through the forest having battled with an ogre, but there was no one else to go. The rest of their friends were huddled around the child and the pack itself was full of half-emaciated captives, only recently freed from those shadowy tunnels themselves.

"I'll come with you," Ellanden said automatically, feeling grateful he'd grabbed that shirt on their way down. "The three of us can handle this."

Evie held up a hand—his bandages were already starting to bleed through.

"You need to *rest*, Ellanden. Ash and I can—"

"Let him come," Asher interrupted.

The fae shot him a grateful look, one that probably had a lot to do with the beautiful witch who was purposely avoiding his eyes. He headed in the opposite direction, waving them along.

"We'll be back soon," Evie assured Seth quietly. "Don't let anyone else down those stairs."

He nodded without looking, eyes fastened on his sister. "Thank you."

"Are you sure you don't want help?" Cosette cast a worried look over her shoulder, though she was reluctant to leave the wolf on his own. "You three just got back—"

"We'll be fine," Evie promised, lowering her voice as she glanced at the shifter. "He needs you here. Stay with them."

Without another word the three friends extracted themselves from the crowd and headed back across the courtyard, arming themselves with whatever random weapons they happened to find along the way. The pack closed ranks around the child, and the last thing Evie saw was Adelaide's look of concern as they pulled open the door to the lower stairwell and vanished from sight.

Chapter 8

As far as 'dangerous missions' went, it wasn't the worst the friends had ever seen.

They walked at a brisk pace down the stairwell, not saying a word until they were out of earshot from the crowd. At that point they made a silent assessment of their weapons, traded a few things around, then kept moving with increasing caution down the darkened steps.

The torches grew smaller and more infrequent. If it weren't for her father's blood racing through her veins, there were places Evie wasn't sure how she would have seen at all.

"They let the children play down here?" she asked incredulously. "How did they even see?"

Asher cast her a quick glance before sliding his hand into hers. "They're all wolves."

That was the last of the talking. That was also the last of the torches. Ellanden grabbed the last one off the wall as they walked by.

Just a few minutes later their footsteps echoed suddenly back to them and they came to a collective pause, peering cautiously at the rounded stone wall. A dead-end. There were indeed a few empty casks of rum, but from the looks of things they had been long since abandoned. There was no fresh ash from a torch, and the only tracks were small enough to belong to children.

After only a brief glance around, they came up at a loss.

"Maybe she was frightened," Ellanden said quietly. "Overexcited herself and collapsed."

Evie nodded slowly, but the vampire wasn't so sure.

His chin lifted ever so slightly, like he was sniffing the breeze. Then he suddenly moved forward, running his fingers along an almost imperceptible crack in the wall.

"Do you see this?" he asked.

The others stepped up beside him, staring down at the stone.

"What is that?" Evie asked curiously, digging her nail into the groove. It was too straight to be accidental, and too even a slice to have been made by anything except a blade.

The men stared a moment longer before Ellanden set the torch aside.

"Help me move it."

Asher nodded swiftly, and together they braced their weight against the floor, digging their fingers into the stone and pushing as hard as they could possibly could.

...nothing happened.

Impressive.

If it wasn't for the seriousness of the situation, the princess would have laughed. For the life of her, she couldn't remember the last time either of the two men had lacked the strength to get something done. All that momentum, all that build-up—only to get bested by a crack in a wall.

"Maybe you should try talking to it," she suggested helpfully.

They deliberately ignored her, throwing themselves into a second try.

Two pairs of boots wedged against the dirt as they forgot the groove entirely and simply slammed their shoulders into the stone. The fae winced involuntarily—judging from the way the vampire's eyes dilated in the dark, fresh blood scented the air—but the two continued on regardless.

Panting quietly, working quietly...then cursing a bit louder than that.

"Seven hells," Ellanden breathed, glancing up towards the ceiling, "are you even pushing?"

It was fortunate he didn't catch the look Asher flashed him in the dark.

"No, I'm reclining," the vampire snapped, lifting his fingers to the wall. "Maybe if we wedged it with a piece of stone, we could get some leverage—"

"We don't need any of that," the fae insisted, offended by the very notion. "If you would just put some strength into it—"

"Hubris," Evie murmured, pretending to examine her nails. "It'll get you every time."

Ellanden flipped her off, while Asher flashed a quick grin.

"Thanks for the support, love."

She nodded sensibly, but when they started at it again she was instantly overcome with boredom—waving the torch at such speeds it was possible she was trying to write her name.

"It doesn't look much bigger than the one you lifted back in Aluthan's Hammer," she said offhandedly. "That time Ellanden was almost crushed to death and you decided to eat him alive."

The fae tensed in spite of himself, and Asher cast a strained look over his shoulder.

"Must you always be so helpful?"

She smiled sweetly. "I'm just trying to figure out what's taking so long."

We had momentum.. Now I'm making shadow-puppets.

"We're trying to move a *wall*," the fae replied shortly, grinding his teeth with the strain. "And one of us has a giant hole in the middle of his chest."

She watched them work with silent amusement.

"I was assured that wasn't a problem. The vampire vouched for you, said you could come."

"He was kissed by a beautiful woman," Asher chided, eyes twinkling in the dark. "He needed to hide below ground. I thought offering him an invitation was the least I could do."

"Give me that torch," Ellanden panted, shouldering his weight against the stone.

Asher extended it at once.

"Why?"

The fae reached blindly for the grip. "Because I'm going to set your hair on fire."

The flames were placed quickly out of reach while the men threw themselves into the task once more. Beads of sweat ran through their hair. Words were clipped and strained. It wasn't until Evie started theatrically snoring that there was a mighty groan and the wall abruptly moved.

...an inch.

"Seven hells!" she gasped in amazement, sweeping forward. A rush of stale air swept out to greet her, the same odd sulfuric smell she'd noticed when they'd first arrived. "I didn't think that would actually work! I didn't think the thing *could* move!"

The fae squinted into the darkness, picking up the torch while the princess promptly began taking off all her clothes. Asher noticed at the last moment, stepping forward in alarm.

"Whoa—what are you doing?"

"I'm shifting," she said practically, kicking off her shoes. "If there really is something down there, my senses will be ten times sharper as a wolf. Not to mention you guys clearly need me to get that wall open the rest of the way. Not that I haven't enjoyed the nine years it took to get this far."

It looked like the vampire wanted to protest but there was an unmistakable logic at play, and if push came to shove he'd rather his girlfriend was equipped with a pair of deadly claws. In the end he merely shielded her from sight, until the girl vanished and a bouncing wolf sprang up in her place.

THAT'S more like it!

She stretched immediately onto her back legs, nuzzling her noise playfully into his hair until he lost all sense of composure and ducked away with a boyish smile.

"I'll never quite get used to that."

Without seeming to think about it he ran his fingers lightly along her forehead, smoothing down the shimmering fur with rhythmic, absentminded strokes.

It felt *incredible*. She growled viciously when he lowered his hand.

"Used to it?" the fae repeated, glancing over his shoulder, "I should hope not." He stared at the princess a moment before gesturing with the torch. "You *slept* with that. If that doesn't trigger some major cognitive dissonance, I don't know what will."

The princess growled, while Asher pushed rudely past him.

"Didn't the last girl you slept with spend most of her life as a tree?"

Ellanden shrugged unapologetically. "She was a woodland nymph. It's a sacred calling."

"A sacred calling," Asher echoed under his breath. "The girl was a glorified deciduous. Let's see if I can manage to make some jokes out of that..."

And let's see if I can make that injury of yours a little more symmetrical—

"Don't bite me."

The princess lifted her eyes to see the fae looking directly at her, holding a silver knife in between. He kept the blade level, staring down in a silent warning, until she finally relented and moved to the gap in the rock. The vampire was already there, straining against the mighty wall.

They took up position on either side of him, throwing their strength against the stone. At least one of them did. Evie waited until Ellanden's hands were busy and he'd sheathed the blade.

Then she licked up the side of his face.

※

ONCE THE FRIENDS HAD finally pried the stone open, there wasn't some great fanfare. No army of demons leapt out to greet them, or anything else that could explain why little Violet had collapsed where she stood. There was nothing but a rush of musty air, followed by a giant cloud of dust.

The trio peered into the darkness, then Evie let out an undignified sneeze.

"Keep it together," Ellanden muttered, still smarting from the lick.

"Bless you," Asher added, tossing her a quick smile as he forced the opening even wider, making enough room for the others to slip past him into the dark.

Seven hells!

Just a few seconds inside and the princess was already regretting her decision to explore the tunnel as a wolf. The added sensitivity wreaked havoc on her nerves already stretched to the brink by the mere question of what new horror might be waiting for them in the shadows.

Her ears pricked forward at the slightest whisper, her fur bristled instinctively the second she touched the ground. Her eyes were strained with the glaring flicker of their single torch and that strange smell was getting worse by the second, creeping inside her over-sensitized nose.

What the hell IS that?

She danced nervously in place, waiting for Asher to join them, cringing instinctively closer to the side of Ellanden's leg. For once, he didn't mind the proximity. In fact he reached down just like Asher had done, scratching her distractedly behind her velvety ears.

"This doesn't make any sense," he murmured, peering into the darkness. "Why would they hollow out space beneath the foundations of such a heavy structure?" His eyes flitted nervously towards the ceiling as tiny particles of dust floated down from above. "There's a bloody moat..."

"You're being paranoid," Asher said calmly, joining them and dusting off his hands. "This place has stood for hundreds of years—there hasn't been a cave-in yet."

...that you know of.

"And the child?" Ellanden asked testily.

The vampire tensed a moment, then stepped bravely down the path.

"That's what we're here to find out..."

By the light of a single torch the friends continued their glacial walk down the stone path, jumping at shadows and growing increasingly disconcerted as that cloying smell intensified with every breath. What had started as a manageable discomfort was soon overwhelming. After a few minutes the princess came to a sudden stop—pawing at the side of her nose with a pitiful whine.

"Trust me," Ellanden breathed, "it wouldn't be better if you were human."

In fact, it looked to be a great deal worse.

The eternally graceful fae was walking with quick, disjointed movements. He was blinking more than necessary and it seemed like all he could do was keep pace.

"Unless something actually came out of this place and attacked the child, I don't see what this has to do with Violet," Asher murmured, taking the torch from Ellanden and lifting it high enough to see. "Although I can't believe...*seven hells*."

The others stopped behind him, staring in wonder by the light of the flame.

The stone pathway they'd been walking stopped abruptly, widening into a gaping cavern that stretched as far as the eye could see. Ellanden was right—they had to be outside the walls of the fortress by now, beneath the forest itself. There would be no room for it otherwise, since the place was massive—a winding labyrinth of caves and tunnels.

"What the heck is this place?" Asher gasped, taking a step forward.

The princess stepped forward with him, scratching tentatively at the wall. It didn't feel like stone. In fact, she wasn't sure it was stone at all. Her claws raked deep grooves into the side, and when she pulled bac, her fur was glistening with the same metallic particles floating in the air.

Ellanden coughed softly and turned his face.

"The slavers couldn't have known this was here," the vampire continued, peering curiously into the dark. Unlike the others, he didn't require the assistance of torchlight. Those glittering eyes were designed to navigate such places with ease. "Neither could the soldiers. A place of such scale has to have a second opening—which would render all their fortifications useless. That means the royal forces didn't construct this place themselves. They must have taken it over at some point."

Evie threw him a quick glance, remembering when he'd said such things before.

I thought it was a garrison. The location, the design...all of that would make sense. But the inside is different. The inside is strange.

"I wonder why they—"

There was a faint shuffling behind him as the fae stumbled back a step—coughing into his sleeve and groping blindly for the wall. His face was shock white and those lovely eyes were rimmed red. Asher turned immediately, sweeping back with the torch held high in his hand.

"Are you okay?"

Ellanden started to nod, then shook his head quickly—backing another step away.

"Can we leave?" He coughed again, struggling to find that immortal poise. "This is worse than—" another cough, "—the mine."

The princess stared at him, then blinked hard—tossing her head as that peculiar scent tickled at her nose. He'd said something, hadn't he? What did he just say?

"Leave?" Asher repeated in surprise, staring with concern as the fae touched the wall for balance. "No, we haven't...we haven't even made it past the first..." He took a step closer, reaching out a hand. "Landi, what's—"

"I can't breathe," the fae said suddenly, stumbling towards the door. His eyes were shining but the lids were heavy, and with every labored breath they threatened to slide shut. "Something isn't right here. I can't...Ash, I can't breathe!"

For a split second, the princess thought he was having a panic attack. All things considered, he was certainly entitled. But he collapsed to the ground a moment later—eyes closed, head rolling to the side, ivory hair splayed out over the cavern floor.

"Ellanden!"

Asher was kneeling beside him in an instant—checking his pulse, feeling for breath. The princess paced nervously, letting out a low whine as his eyes tightened in concentration.

Whatever he determined, it wasn't good.

"Get him outside!"

Without the slightest hesitation, she grabbed the fae by the back of the shirt and dragged him in a full-sprint towards the opening of the tunnel. His legs trailed lifelessly behind, and she was hyper-aware of every time his body knocked against the jagged rocks. But she didn't need to be a vampire to hear the fae's heartbeat. It was getting slower with each second they spent below ground.

Asher had passed them and was already waiting by the time they got to the exit, clutching one of those strange rocks in his free hand. The other was pressed hard against the entrance to the tunnel, wedging it open just far enough to let them both sail through.

It swung shut the moment they were safely inside, but the vampire didn't follow them and the princess didn't stop moving. While she bolted up the stairwell—those deadly teeth embedded in the prince's tunic—he started grabbing the empty rum casks and stacking them in front of the stone, ripping off his jacket and stuffing it into the crack for good measure when he was through.

Please wake up...please wake up...

Evie streaked through the corridor and out into the main courtyard, relieved that the pack had moved their impromptu gathering somewhere inside. A lone shifter flashed a curious look as she tore past, but she flew across the drawbridge and into the woods with no further interference, slowing to a breathless stop the second she was hidden within the trees.

Please, Ellanden! Please wake up!

Asher was right—how many more times could they keep doing this? How many times could they break before they were unable to piece themselves back together? The fae had been stabbed that very morning, had fought an ogre that very afternoon. The man was still bleeding from the freaking bear trap, let alone whatever damage the slavers had done when she'd been unconscious!

What the hell were we thinking?! Why did we let him come along?!

As delicately as possible, she lowered him to the ground—unclenching her teeth before giving him a gentle nudge. There was a swish of air and Asher appeared beside, tossing over her clothes as she quickly transformed and got dressed, kneeling a second later by the fae's side.

"Ellanden?" she said softy, giving him a gentle shake.

Nothing happened.

"No one can get down there," Asher murmured, tapping anxiously on the prince's face with the tips of his fingers. "It's completely blocked off."

She nodded silently, fighting back tears.

The only reason she wasn't straight-up screaming was that the fae still had a pulse. It wasn't getting stronger, but it wasn't getting weaker either. All they could do now was wait.

...not the vampire's forte.

"Has he moved, or anything?" he pressed, shaking the prince quite a bit more roughly than she had done herself. "Is there any—"

But at that moment, Ellanden woke up with a gasp—raising a hand in front of him as if warding off phantoms the others couldn't see. His eyes flew around the forest in confusion, pupils shrinking in the sudden light as he pulled in quick, uneven breaths, like he might not get another.

"What happened?" he panted, spinning with disorientation. A tightened fist pressed against the blanket of pine needles, holding up his weight. "I can't—"

"We pulled you out from the..." Evie trailed off, worried beyond what was reasonable and gripping his other hand. "Ellanden, you couldn't breathe in the..."

She trailed off again, struck by the sudden simplicity.

It wasn't a crack in the foundation or a mystery beneath the forest any more than it was a quirk in design. The hidden cavern was much simpler than that. And much more obvious.

Her eyes drifted to the heap of sparkling rock in Asher's hand.

"It's a terium mine."

"I'M RIGHT."

The princess looked between her two friends, repeating the assertion for the second time. It hadn't gotten far. Especially given its less-than-receptive audience.

The prince of the fae was remote, staring with the enchanting eyes of someone who might have been gifted with celestial beauty but was currently undergoing repairs. While the vampire was silently calculating how many wine casks it would take to stop whatever dangerous substance was leaking into the fortress from those haunting caverns.

He just hadn't realized it was terium.

"You think it was—"

"Think about it," the princess interrupted, suddenly eager now that she knew one of her best friends was merely sedated. "The guard at the gate was thrilled that you'd brought people as vibrant as Freya and Cosette, because most prisoners were 'sickly kids from the village that didn't last more than a few days'. But that doesn't make any sense, does it? Because the children from Seth's village are survivors. They grew up in the mountains—they're strong. It wasn't the guards or the slavers who were making them unwell—it was the terium leaching up through the ground."

Ellanden stared a moment longer, then his eyes drifted to the shimmering rock.

"...put it down."

Asher dropped it in a heartbeat, kicking it away for good measure. The princess still had a smear on her wrist, and while she did nothing to test the theory she was sure that if it had gotten even a little closer to her face she would have been sprawled out on the ground, same as the fae.

"I thought they were all destroyed," Asher said quietly. "The mines. I thought the Damaris king destroyed them before the terium could be used against him and his armies."

"They *were* destroyed," Ellanden answered, pushing onto his elbows. "At least...they were supposed to be. My father told me terium is incredibly rare. To have found an entire mine..."

He trailed off as each of them considered it for the first time.

There were endless possibilities, none of them very good. There was a reason such potent weapons had been eliminated from both sides, and a massive body-count to support that reason.

"Do you think we should even tell anyone?" Evie asked tentatively, staring hard at the other two. "I mean, we'll make sure no one goes down there. But this stuff..." Her eyes drifted to the piece Asher had recovered, glittering amidst a tangle of ferns. "It can be deadly. Even an accidental dose can be deadly. Healers stopped using it long before the mines were destroyed."

Asher considered it thoughtfully. Ellanden was still trying to keep himself awake.

"We have to tell the others," the vampire concluded, "and Seth will want to tell the rest of his pack. To be honest, I can't blame him. If they're going to be living right on top of the thing, they deserve to know what's down there. We can tell the elders, let them do what they think is best."

Evie nodded, secretly relieved that for once the decision wasn't in their hands. She turned her attention instead to the fae—who was in the process of pushing himself off the ground.

"Nope!"

She was by his side a moment later, easing him back down. To her surprise, Asher was right across from her, doing the exact same thing.

"You're done playing hero," she said quietly, giving his shoulder a quick squeeze. "The only thing in your immediate future is a bed, do you hear me?"

"She's right," Asher echoed before he could respond. "No argument."

The prince glanced between them, searching for the weaker link.

"No heroics," he teased. "I was just trying to sit—"

"And tomorrow you wanted to go hunting," Evie interrupted. "And fishing, and hiking around the forest, searching for your new bow." She gave him another squeeze, afraid of doing it too hard. "You need to *rest*, Landi. We both do. These things come at a cost."

Her eyes drifted down the weathered trail, where her grandmother's house had recently burned to the ground—taking an entire lifetime with it. Almost claiming theirs in the process.

"We need to stop pretending they don't."

The fae opened his mouth to argue, but for once it looked like he was too exhausted to put up much of a fight. The most he did was shrug out of their grasp, muttering a petulant, "You know my kind are excellent healers. Just one of our many strengths."

Asher graciously hid a smile, while Evie bit down on her lip.

I have an idea where this is going...

When neither of them said anything, his pulse quickened with rising panic.

"A wound like this is nothing to a fae," he continued heatedly, silently begging one of them to speak. "My father once scaled Redfern Peak after having survived a bloody avalanche. You can't put a price on that kind of endurance. We bounce back. We're virtually indestructible..."

He trailed off miserably, glancing between them with a sigh.

"Was I the only one that...you know..."

"Fainted?" Asher asked with a grin.

Evie snorted into her sleeve, while Ellanden literally paled with an impotent kind of rage.

"Don't say that word," he commanded. "Call it something else."

Asher nodded seriously. "Something other than fainting?"

Ellanden winced like he'd drawn a blade. "Blacked out. Say I blacked out."

"No one needs to say anything," Evie interjected diplomatically. Most days such torments were a favorite pastime, but she was feeling irrationally protective. "We discovered there was a mine and blocked off the entrance. That's the only thing anyone has to know—"

"But it was just me?" the fae pressed, staring with quiet desperation between them. "Neither of you—"

"Neither of us was human," Evie interrupted. They used the word loosely. Growing up in the five kingdoms, you kind of had to. "I had shifted into a wolf and Asher is technically *dead*."

She said the word sharply. A punishment for *fainting*.

"You remember when our parents were dosed with terium on that ship," she added. "It took far more to make Uncle Aidan fall asleep."

Both of them glanced at Asher, who shrugged with a broad grin.

"Just impossibly strong, I guess."

Not helping.

Whether he was feeling protective himself or correctly interpreted the arctic glare upon her face, the vampire quit his teasing as well—slipping his hands behind Ellanden's back and helping him carefully to his feet. When the fae swayed precariously, he caught him quickly by the shoulder.

"You okay?" he asked with concern. "Feeling a little—"

"What—*faint*?" the fae snapped, yanking himself away. "Were you going to say *faint*?"

Asher lifted his hands peaceably. "I was going to say, 'blacked out.'"

BY THE TIME THE TRIO of friends made it back to the fortress, the rest of the pack had already gone to sleep. Even Adelaide had retired for the night, though she'd left clear instructions for the others to wake her if they didn't come back within the hour. When they crossed the drawbridge and trudged wearily through the gate, only three people were sitting in the center of the courtyard.

"There you are," Cosette called with relief. "We were about to head out and search."

Freya stayed just long enough to see they were safe, then pushed silently to her feet and headed back to her room. Ellanden stared painfully after her, then bowed his head with a quiet sigh.

"How's your sister?" Evie asked Seth immediately, settling beside them on the wet stones.

The fortress might have provided enough rooms for everyone present, but they were still accustomed to sleeping together. And there was something innately calming about the cool night air.

"She came out of it a few minutes after you left," Seth replied, looking visibly relieved. His fingers were laced casually with Cosette's—a recent development neither of them seemed to have noticed themselves. "Tell me you found out what happened."

Asher nodded tiredly, dark hair spilling into his eyes.

"We did—but you won't like it. Turns out this entire fort is built on a terium mine."

There was a beat of silence.

"...a what?"

To those gifted with immortality, ten years was a drop in the ocean. But there were certain moments when it felt like a very long time. The idea of terium had faded with the practice, and those who remembered its sting had been wiped out along with what remained of the mines. The only reason the friends were familiar with the term was from their parents' stories.

"It's a sedative," Cosette said softly, having been raised on the same tales herself. "A very powerful one—dangerous and imprecise. It was also said to have been destroyed." She lifted her eyes curiously to the others. "Are you sure it was terium?"

For a split second, they were silent.

Two fought hard to hold back a smile. The third simply froze.

"Yep."

"Absolutely sure."

"Positive."

Seth looked between them, deciding not to press.

"Okay, well...should we evacuate the fort?" he asked tentatively. "If it's as dangerous as you say, I can't imagine—"

"The fort's been in use for decades," Ellanden interrupted curtly, eyeing their joined hands. "No one's had a problem with it until now, and that's just because they were keeping people in the dungeon, near the entrance of the mine. Seal off the lower levels, and everyone should be fine."

The shifter looked at him nervously, but nodded. "If you're sure—"

"I am."

Asher glanced between them, then pushed abruptly to his feet.

"We have rooms in this place, we have beds. Let's use them." He offered a hand down to the princess, eyes twinkling with a secret smile. "Let's not waste this time."

She took it with a grin as the rest of them stood up beside her—glancing up at the moonlit stone as they tried to remember which chambers had been assigned to them.

"Did you hear that?" Evie stretched onto her toes, speaking directly into Ellanden's ear. "I'm reminding the man who was recently *stabbed*...he's under orders to stay in bed tomorrow."

He muttered something under his breath, and her eyes sharpened dangerously.

"I'd be happy to talk a little more about that mine..."

There was a beat of silence, then he forced a cheerful wave.

"I'll be in bed tomorrow if anyone needs me. Pleasant dreams."

He was gone before the others could say a word, ghosting up the stairs whilst casting fearful looks back at the princess. She held his gaze until the moment he disappeared inside before heading off with the others, climbing to the corridor on the other side of the square.

"How did you know we were in the forest?" she asked suddenly, wondering why they were waiting in the courtyard instead of down in the tunnels.

Cosette glanced back with a curious smile.

"One of the shifters said he saw a wolf streak through here, dragging what looked to be a dolled-up corpse." She paused for effect. "Anything you'd like to add?"

Evie and Asher exchanged a quick glance.

"Nope."

"Must have been out of his mind."

Chapter 9

The friends had agreed to take it easy for a day. They stayed in bed for the next three.

It was an extravagance they hadn't allowed themselves since running away from the royal caravan—the time to catch their breath, the time to heal. They had attempted it once before with Evianna, but there was only so much one could recuperate in a swamp. The fortress was different.

After ten years sleeping on a damp cave floor, followed by the subsequent weeks spent fighting monsters and trekking through the wilderness, there was no putting a price on something so simple as a bed. A room. A place to stay with a locked door. And a drawbridge. And a moat.

Once the initial shock wore off and the princess was able to let her guard down, she was perfectly willing to remain there until the inevitable end of days.

Perhaps they would initiate her into the pack. Perhaps she could head up a hunting brigade or dedicate herself to a life of laundry, in exchange for the simple luxury of getting to sleep.

The only time she left her bedroom was to have dinner with Adelaide—a woman who was taking the opportunity to slowly acclimate back into the real world. The days were spent helping at the fort, or wandering in the forest. Interactions were kept to a minimum, but there were more every day. The evenings were spent having supper with the princess—telling stories, sharing sentimental moments, catching up on everything they'd missed. On the third night, Cosette joined them.

But the days...the days belonged to Asher.

And he was determined not to waste a second.

"Hold still."

The princess squirmed and giggled, shoulder blades pressed to the mattress as Asher held her ankle in the air—trailing slow kisses up the inside of her leg. A flaming blush burned her cheeks as she watched him get higher and higher. Those dark eyes were staring right back, locked onto hers.

"Hold still, I said." He pressed his lips to the back of her knee, eyes twinkling when she squirmed in spite of herself, hands fisting around the sheet. "I'll have to start from the beginning..."

Sounds good to me.

"We wouldn't want that," she panted, trying her best to stop moving.

It wasn't easy. The man was naked.

She didn't think she'd ever get used to it—the sight of him like that. The first day he'd taken off his clothes, she'd frozen on the spot. Four mornings later, she'd yet to catch her breath.

He was perfection. Absolute perfection.

And he's all mine.

The princess' eyes lit up as her mind travelled back to the night before, silently reveling in the memory. Instead of being paralyzed by that naked body, she'd taken her time...exploring.

Between all of her friends, Asher was the quiet one. He was much like his father in that regard. Reserved, soft-spoken, with a sudden withering sense of humor.

Imagine her delight upon discovering she could make him scream.

There were so many memories to choose from, she didn't know where to start. Every time he arched his back, every time he cried out with reckless abandon. But even better were the quiet moments, the secret whispers. She loved making him smile. She loved making him blush.

That morning, he was determined to return the favor.

"Hold *still*," he insisted, pushing her down without the slightest bit of effort.

The past few days had been full of silent revelations, and that strength of his had been one of the greatest. She realized now how careful he was with the rest of them at all times. Even with Ellanden. Fae were strong in their own right, but it didn't really compare to a vampire.

He continued that line of dizzying kisses, but came to a pause at her thigh. His eyes sparked with mischief as his tongue snuck out. At the same time, his teeth lightly grazed her skin.

"At this point...you'll want to hold *very* still."

He had bitten her there only once, the first night they spent together. At the same time, she had tasted his own blood. It was a level of intensity for which neither had been quite prepared.

And I'm in no state to handle it now.

"My turn."

Once Evie learned there was simply no overpowering him, she'd developed an alternative strategy to get her way. She showered him with kisses instead.

"*Your* turn?" He pulled back with a burst of laughter, reaching out instinctively as she threw her body into the air. "I was just getting started!"

She flashed a devilish smile, landing in his arms.

"And now I want my turn."

He laughed again in surprise, falling onto the bed as she crawled into his lap and wrapped her legs around his waist. His fingers tightened on her back, ready as always, but she took her time, teasing him the same way he'd been doing since she opened her eyes that morning.

When he tried to sit up, she eased him back down—whispering a kiss into the hollow of his neck, the exact place where he'd bitten her the night before. His breathing hitched and those dark eyes closed as he reclined onto the pillow, bathed in a soft halo of morning light.

For a suspended moment, she merely stared at him—marveling in silence at his face. It was almost unreal. Like a dark angel who'd fallen from the heavens and found his way into her bed.

BLESSING

"What's wrong?"

She jerked out of her trance to see him staring at her, a silent question in his eyes. Instead of answering she leaned forward and kissed him, deciding at the last moment to add a little bite.

His lips curved into a smile as he tossed his head playfully, trying to shake her loose.

"I've warned you about biting before, princess. You won't win."

"Oh yeah?" She arched her eyebrow, preparing her attack—then recanted at the last second and rolled onto her side. "Actually...I'm starving."

He pulled back in surprise, looking her up and down.

Like he'd forgotten a world existed outside their bedroom. Like he'd forgotten not everyone could subsist on blood alone—that mortals needed food and water and sunshine to survive.

"Of course," he said suddenly, leaping to his feet. His clothes were scattered all over the room—he'd yet to find them since that first night—but he hurried back and forth with no particular direction, throwing on random things as he went. "I'm so sorry, I was distracted and...and I should pay better attention to those sorts of things." He paused with a tunic pulled halfway over his head, turning around to face her. "Shall I get you something? I can always—"

She stepped in front of him with a smile, catching his frantic hands. As she'd yet to find any clothes of her own, it was rather counterproductive. His eyes swept her up and down before heating with that simmering impatience she had grown to love so well.

"It's fine. I can get something myself—"

"Are you sure you're hungry?" he interrupted, tracing a finger along her collarbone. A little smile tugged at the corner of his lips. "What if I could take your mind off it?" That finger slid down to her wrist, pulling her causally to the bed. "What if I—"

"Is this a kidnapping?"

He stopped cold. "...what?"

She spoke with a perfect calm, staring directly at him. "You starving me, keeping me against my will? It's starting to feel like a kidnapping."

There was a beat of guilty silence. Then his face cleared with an innocent smile.

"It's not a kidnapping at all. We're going to get...breakfast."

She stretched onto her toes and kissed his cheek. "That's the spirit."

And on that note...

Despite all the time they'd spent together the last few months, it had been almost impossible to get any time alone. A shared tent wasn't the most erotic place to get things started, not with four of their friends sleeping nearby, and they'd taken full advantage of their newfound privacy.

...at the expense of the room.

"Okay—breakfast." Evie glanced around helplessly, shoving tangled hair from her eyes. "If I can find my clothes. *If* you haven't torn straight through them." She paused nervously, biting her lower lip. "...was that dresser broken when we got here?"

That gentle, soft-spoken reserve? Turns out there was a whole other side to him. One that didn't play so well with things like furniture and women's clothes.

He flushed ever so slightly, then brightened with a sudden idea.

"Actually, take your time." He came up behind her, easing back her curling hair and weaving it into a loose braid. She froze in surprise, electrified by every grazing sweep of his fingers. When he finished, he twirled her around with a twinkling smile. "Let me worry about breakfast. You just relax up here...wander down whenever you're ready."

Her eyebrows rose slowly as she considered what that might mean.

"Ash...you know we eat different things, right?" An image of a screaming rodent drowning in a swamp flashed through her mind. "You know mine require things like cooking...not catching?"

His lips quirked up in a dry smile.

"Having spent my entire life with mortals, I'm pretty clear on what they eat. Thanks."

"Just making sure."

On that note, he kissed her on the forehead—lingering in spite of himself before sweeping away with a smile. The door swung open, and he glanced over his shoulder with a wink.

"Leave it to me."

Famous last words.

WHEN THE PRINCESS WANDERED down to the kitchen about twenty minutes later, the vampire had yet to make much progress. Mostly because, while he might be familiar with the different things that mortals ate, he had no idea how to go about making such things himself.

He'd paced back and forth, too embarrassed to ask any of the shifters for help, but he leapt to his feet with renewed enthusiasm when Ellanden wandered into the room.

"Hey—I need a favor."

The fae glanced at him in surprise, lingering on the flush to his skin and that radiant smile always on the corners of his lips. He stared a moment, then moved to the cabinets with a secret grin.

"I can't believe you're here," he answered. "The rest of us had bets going as to whether we'd ever see either of you again. That being said, I've certainly *heard* you..." he added under his breath.

The Prince of the Fae might have resisted the idea of bed rest with every fiber of his being, but it had clearly done him wonders. There was finally some color to his face and an ease to the way he was moving that hadn't been there in a long time.

"On that note, I'm not sure what favors *I* could possibly do for you, Ash." He glanced over his shoulder with a wicked grin. "But I'm sure if you asked Evie—"

The vampire appeared directly in front of him. "I need you to teach me how to cook."

Evie melted against the wall with a grin, watching in the reflection of an open window.

Oh, COME on.

The fae blinked in surprise. "Like...food?"

Asher nodded enthusiastically, prompting a sparkling laugh. The fae looked at him fondly, then raked back his hair—glancing around the kitchen. Ironically enough, he was better suited to a campfire than a stove. Growing up, he'd always had servants for that sort of thing.

"I don't know much—"

"You know more than me."

Ellanden laughed again, unaccustomed to seeing such a side to him.

"Okay, sure." He pulled a cup from the cabinet, filling it with a steaming brew. "Before we leave, we can find a time to—"

The cup was taken from his hand.

"Oh—now?"

Asher nodded again, throwing an anxious glance at the stairs.

"Really quick—before Evie comes down."

The fae pursed his lips with an affectionate smile, then agreed—taking his cup back in the process. With a grand gesture he waved Asher to the grill, lighting it to boil some water.

"You get that since we left Evie has been eating primarily squirrel, right?"

There was a pointed silence.

"Can you please suppress all those charming instincts and do me this favor?" the vampire asked sharply. "Considering all the favors I've done for you in the past?"

Ellanden shot him a sideways glance, then continued with the kettle. "That's hard to argue..."

Without further ado, the two men set themselves to work.

The fae was no master himself, but he knew the basics—frying an egg, warming some toast, slicing some fruit to arrange on the side. The bulk of the lesson consisted of him showing Asher the spice cabinet, then telling him to stay very far away.

The vampire absorbed the lesson with wide eyes, memorizing each movement and placing everything they'd assembled on a tray. It wasn't until Ellanden plucked a flower from the windowsill and pulled down another cup that he peered over his shoulder with a question.

"What's that?"

"Jasmine," the fae replied, shredding the petals absentmindedly and dropping them into the glass. Asher looked up blankly and he continued, "Evie loves jasmine tea. It's her favorite."

The hint of a frown shadowed across the vampire's face as sweet steam rose into the air.

"How did *you* know that, but not me?" he murmured.

Ellanden shrugged carelessly, placing it on the tray. "Because she's always stealing mine." He glanced up, looking unexpectedly grave. "You're dating a *monster*, Asher. You need to feed that monster jasmine tea."

Evie rolled her eyes with a grin, then jumped forward as Seth came down the stairs.

"Hang on," she whispered, grabbing his sleeve. "Don't go in there just yet."

The shifter raised his eyebrows, speaking in a theatric whisper himself.

"And why not?"

"We're doing a social experiment," she breathed, gesturing to the window. "Introducing a vampire to the wonders of human food."

Seth glanced inside, then leaned beside her with a grin. "This could take all day…"

They listened as what started as a rational conversation about utensils dissolved into a full-fledged shouting match over what constituted a 'civilized society' as Ellanden waved a fork.

Freya breezed downstairs a moment later, pausing curiously when she saw the others hiding against the wall. That curiosity intensified when a dinner roll flew into the courtyard.

"What are we doing?"

"Social experiment," Evie replied, flinching at what sounded like a slap.

"Breakfast by osmosis," Seth clarified. "We're hoping that if we stand very still..."

He trailed off as the final member of their party swept downstairs, looking incomparably lovely as the morning sunlight glinted off her ivory hair. Instead of her usual warrior's braid it was hanging in loose waves down her shoulders, with a tiny star-shaped flower tucked above her ear.

Seth's eyes alighted on the flower, twinkling with a secret smile. "Good morning."

Only someone watching closely could have seen Cosette blush.

"Good morning," she replied innocently. "Are we getting some breakfast?"

Evie's eyes danced with amusement.

"We most certainly are—"

A sudden hush fell over the kitchen.

"Evie?" Asher called in a panic.

Crap.

It was a testament to the vampire's mental state that he hadn't noticed her lurking there already. There was a chance Ellanden had, but the fae magnanimously decided not to say anything.

That gracious silence ended the moment she stepped inside.

"Come see what our vampire whipped up for breakfast." He nudged Asher forward, placing the tray in his hands. "All by himself, too—the little warrior. There's nothing this guy can't do."

Asher blushed furiously as Freya took a sudden step back.

The three-day respite might have been heaven for the others, but it had done nothing to help the young witch. She was pale and jittery, and judging by the darkened hollows beneath her eyes there had been very little sleep. There was, however, a grim determination.

"I'm not really hungry," she muttered, turning back to the stairs.

Cosette looked after her in concern.

"Frey—"

"I'm fine." The witch flashed a tight smile. "Just going back to my room."

The fae took another step after her, then realized it was hopeless and let out a little sigh.

While they might have assimilated into a larger group the two girls had started the adventure together, travelling for years by each other's sides. They'd scaled mountains and hunted monsters, navigated awkward parental check-ins and watched each other's backs in crowded taverns where half the patrons were armed and the other half was trying to buy them a drink.

They knew when to press and when to hold back. They also knew precisely what it would take for that delicate balance to break. For the last three days...Freya had been there.

"Do you want to go after her?" Seth murmured under his breath.

Cosette shook her head tiredly. "No...I'll bring her something later."

They headed inside to where the men were waiting obliviously, reveling in the success of the vampire's first venture into the culinary world. A breathtaking display that consisted of...

...burnt toast and eggs.

Evie's eyes swept over the tray.

"Ash, that's...that's awesome." She beamed up at him, praying to the heavens he wouldn't see anything suspicious behind the smile. "Thank you so much!"

The others froze behind her, but the vampire flushed with pride.

"It's no big deal." He gestured to the mug. "I know how you like tea..."

She nodded quickly, taking a scalding gulp.

"I certainly do."

And I certainly DON'T like that.

The tray turned out to be a bit superfluous as everyone gathered around the table together, but the princess kept it anyway—picking her way carefully through the plate as Asher pretended not to be watching from the corner of his eye.

"It's so good," she said for the fifth time, washing down a mouthful of smoked bread with another burning gulp of tea. Ellanden's eyes twinkled and she flashed a saccharine smile. "I *love* it."

The vampire beamed, taking her hand beneath the table as Cosette snuck a bite to see for herself. She blanched but choked it down as well, offering a polite smile.

"Certainly better than the moose you served up in the mountains."

"I would have eaten that raw," Ellanden said, stretching his arms. If memory served, they basically did. "I still can't believe you were able to find that thing. We would have starved for sure."

Asher shrugged casually. "Just a natural in the kitchen, I guess."

The princess spat a piece of ash into Seth's napkin.

"So what's the plan here?" the shifter asked, shooting her a revolted look before tossing the thing into the trash. "Everything sort of came to a standstill after we found out about..."

Kaleb.

No one seemed willing to say his name.

At least...no one's willing to say it to me.

The princess remembered Asher and Ellanden's secret conversation on the best ways to kill a dragon. Even now, a hush fell over the table and no one could seem to meet her gaze.

"Look, it's not some secret," she muttered, jabbing at her plate. "So the man is my uncle. A relative of mine is responsible for single-handedly destabilizing the entire realm. Big surprise."

Always best to discuss these things over breakfast.

Cosette nudged her sympathetically. "He's my uncle, too."

"Yes," Evie agreed, "but everyone likes you more than me."

"...that's true."

"Shouldn't we wait to discuss this until..." Ellanden trailed off, glancing hopefully at the entrance before turning a bit nervously to Cosette. "Do you know if Freya is coming?"

The fae's eyes cooled dangerously. "Why do you care?"

He flinched and fell silent.

"We can't wait to discuss it at all," Asher interjected, still gripping the princess' hand. "As much as I'm grateful for our time here, we have a name now. We have a...a target."

Evie flashed him a quick look.

As much as it stung, she was grateful someone at least had the courage to say the word out loud. Kaleb might have been blood, but he was also the enemy. And if there was one thing growing up a Damaris in the five kingdoms had taught her: enemy beats blood.

But that relief passed as quickly as it had come, leaving her cold and shaken.

"We have a target that we can't possibly hope to destroy," she murmured.

Everyone heard her quite clearly, but Seth felt the need to recant.

"Surely there's *something* we can—"

"What?" Evie challenged. "Do you have a brilliant way to kill a dragon? Much less a dragon that big?" Her eyes flashed to the others. "You should ask *these* two. They were up late discussing it one night."

Ellanden flushed at the table, while Asher pursed his lips.

"I told you," he said mildly, "we were talking about fishing."

Fishing for dragons.

She yanked her hand away reflexively, then grabbed hold of him again—choking down another bite of toast in the process.

"I'm serious," she insisted. "How are we supposed to get past this? Of all the enemies the prophecy could have named...a *sorcerer* with the power of a *dragon*?"

"That's just like Alwyn," Ellanden said quietly. "Our parents managed to beat him."

"Whatever Alwyn transformed into was much, *much* smaller than what we're talking about now," she replied with a shiver. "I told you—I've never seen such a beast."

A thoughtful silence fell over the table.

At a glance, their solution was simple. Find the stone. Without the power of such a talisman, a dragon was just a dragon—no matter how great the size. But a part of them was worried it wasn't so simple. *Get to the Dunes.* The words had been chasing them from one corner of the realm to the next. No matter how many times they tried to get there, the fates threw something new in their path.

And if the dragon could simply fly there on his own? What chance did they have?

"I can't help but think we're forgetting something very important." Seth leaned back in his chair, those dark eyes locked on the princess. "Kaleb might have mixed blood—a dragon with a sorcerer—but Evie, you're a mix of things as well. Your father is the most famous wolf in all the realm. Your bloodline was chosen to wield the stones. Surely that has to give you a leg up."

That's something, I guess...a dragon and a wolf.

Evie considered it a moment, then whispered fearfully:

"What if I'm just a regular dragon...but covered in fur."

There was a beat of silence.

"That would be grotesque," Seth finally answered.

"What about me?" Cosette asked playfully. "I have mixed blood, too. Half-dragon, half-fae."

"Yours would be more graceful," the shifter said authoritatively. "It would also be rude."

Ellanden flashed him a glare across the table as Adelaide walked into the room. Her cheerful smile faded as she saw the faces in front of her. A moment later she glanced at the grill.

"Did something burn?"

Asher's eyes darted to the tray as Evie pushed to her feet with a forced smile.

"Not at all. We were just eating breakfast and discussing...the next steps."

Careful words. If people were walking on eggshells with the princess, they were most certainly doing the same thing with the queen.

Fortunately, Evie had already discussed the matter at great length with Adelaide—not that they'd found a lot of common ground. The queen's first impulse was to find her children. Her next impulse was to assemble an army to handle the threat themselves. Considering she'd fallen in love with a wizard, the woman put no stock whatsoever in the idea of a prophecy. Nor did she think they should adhere to its message, not when those words could endanger her grandchildren's lives.

"So you're still fixed on handling this yourself?" she asked sharply. "Am I to understand this is the kind of monarch you intend to become? The kind that rides at the front of the army? That charges headfirst into battle, willing to give your life for the people fighting at your side?"

The others sat up a bit straighter, but the princess never broke her gaze.

"Like my mother taught me."

Adelaide's lips curved with the hint of a smile.

"I'd expect nothing less. But you still have a lot to learn..."

Chapter 10

The theory was simple: to fight a dragon, one needed to be a dragon.

The reality was somewhat more complicated.

"I've told you a thousand times myself," Ellanden said as the friends headed across the courtyard. "If you want to learn something new, you need to start by taking off your clothes."

Evie shot him a fierce look, then elbowed Asher out of a smile.

I've been hearing that a lot lately.

The others had leapt firmly aboard the whole 'leave it to Everly' idea, and were making no attempt whatsoever to hide their delight. Cosette had stolen something less toxic from the kitchen and headed up to Freya's room, while Seth had fished a bottle of rum from the cabinets and was taking leisurely sips as he strode with them across the stones.

"Are you serious with that?" Evie snapped, instead of answering the fae. "It's, like, nine in the morning, Seth. Isn't your debauched day-drinking reserved as a conflict-avoidance strategy?"

He gestured between them with the bottle. "What do you think this is?"

She ground her teeth together, counting measured breaths.

All her life she'd craved this kind of adventure, drooling over the heroes in her fairytales and dreaming of the day when she might join their hallowed ranks. All her life she'd prepared for the day she might receive her own prophecy, following her mother's legacy and saving the realm.

...she just hadn't imagined doing it naked.

"This is a ridiculous waste of time," she muttered, dragging her feet the closer they got to the gate. "Since I was about three years old, I've tried shifting into a dragon. It has *never* worked. It has never even *begun* to work. Now we're staking the fate of the five kingdoms upon it?"

"There are four kingdoms," Seth reminded her, taking another swig. "Try to keep up. And yes, princess—you've summarized it perfectly. That's exactly what we decided over breakfast."

"There are *five* kingdoms," Asher countered evenly before winding a gentle arm around her shoulders. "And surely you had to know this would come up," he prompted softly, quoting the lines she'd said a thousand times before. "'Peace will prevail if the dragon can fly'? Who's the dragon?"

"Maybe the prophecy meant Kaleb," Ellanden teased. "Maybe he turns good."

Evie shot him another glare.

"Maybe it meant Cosette," she countered, wiping the smile off his face. "I'm not the only one with Damaris blood and the power to turn into a dragon."

The fae hesitated a moment, then cleared his expression.

"You found the prophecy. You dreamt of Kaleb. You were the one who climbed like a monkey all over the castle, dragging the rest of us along. This is up to you, Everly. Get over it."

She shot him a disbelieving look.

"If it helps, I agree with you," he continued graciously. "You're nowhere *near* prepared."

I need to find better friends...

When they reached the gate, both Seth and Ellanden turned to go back. Only Asher had volunteered to stay as she attempted the transformation. Partially because of the nudity. Partially because he got the feeling she might want some company after she dug her fingernails into his hand.

"And where do you think *you're* going?" she demanded, whirling around.

Both men froze mid-step at the look on her face.

"This is why I drink," Seth muttered, raising his hand with a cheerful wave. "You have no need for a wolf, Your Highness. I'd be of much better use up here...guarding the fort."

She rolled her eyes.

Guarding the liquor cabinet.

"And what about you, shape-shifter?" she demanded. "You don't think that would come in handy? Your mother can brew potions and cast spells. You don't think *that* would come in handy?"

The fae froze in surprise, no idea what to say.

Fortunately, the princess wasn't giving him a chance to say anything.

"Nope. If I'm doing this you're doing it, too."

Seth chuckled and clapped him on the shoulder, leaving him to it—while Ellanden glanced wistfully back towards the fortress, pausing on the edge of the bridge.

"And what about Asher?" he accused. "Do you have any unrealistic demands to make of him as well?"

Evie looked the vampire up and down, then gave him an adoring smile. "He's perfect just the way he is."

"What?!" Ellanden cried, Asher smirking behind him. "That's completely—"

"You're perfect, baby. Just stand there and look pretty."

The fae looked between them with a withering glare. "This new thing between you two...I hate it."

Evie beamed as he stalked across the drawbridge, knocking into her shoulder before he vanished into the woods. "He can even cook!"

<hr>

UNWILLING TO BE COMPLETELY naked in front of Ellanden, the princess had compromised. She was draped in Asher's cloak and facing the forest, paling in horror at even the slightest breeze.

"What if it blows off?" she asked for the third time.

Ellanden sighed impatiently and Asher elbowed him in the side.

"It'll be fine, honey. Just focus on—"

"Everly Rose, I have been *living* in the woods with you for the last ten years. Do you really think there's even the slightest chance that I'm interested?"

There was a pause.

"What the heck is THAT supposed to mean?!"

The fae sighed again, rubbing his eyes. "Royalty is so easily offended..."

"Coming from *you*," Asher answered coolly before turning back to his girlfriend. "Honey, I know you can do this. You just need to take a deep breath and relax."

"Ash, I'm trying—"

"Try to put everything else from your mind. There's no pressure, no stress."

"That's easy for you to—"

Ellanden threw up his hands.

"The fate of the kingdoms hangs in the balance!"

There was another awkward pause, then Asher turned with strained patience to the fae.

"You—wait over there. And you..." He appeared in front of Evie a moment later, resting both hands on her shoulders as the prince stalked petulantly into the woods. "...talk to me."

Not 'what's the problem?' Not 'why have you made us stand in the woods for twenty minutes?' Just...'talk to me'. Evie intended to spend the rest of her life doing exactly that.

"I just feel like it's never going to happen," she said softly, watching as the fae's ivory hair moved slowly through the trees. "All these years I've been trying, with my mother helping me, and I've never even come close. And now with all this pressure, with everything at stake—"

"You've transformed under pressure before," he interrupted calmly, sliding his hands down until they were holding hers. "You transformed into a wolf to save Ellanden's life. You tapped into that fire to save mine. Pressure is your friend here, you can't hide from it."

"A wolf is so much different than a dragon," she argued lamely, unable to keep it from sounding like a whine. "It's something manageable. But a dragon—"

"I don't know a man, woman, or child in the five kingdoms who would call the wolves of Belaria manageable," Asher countered gently. "And if it's a matter of avoiding all those doomsday hypotheticals, we can find a way to make it more immediate, more personal."

She shook her head in confusion. "Like how?"

"You want me to attack Ellanden again?" he asked in earnest. "Because I would sincerely be more than happy to—"

"That would be *perfect*. Thanks."

The two of them laughed quietly, but it soon faded from their faces. His was understanding, hers was unsure. After a few seconds, she turned back to the woods.

"I can't beat him," she said frankly. "Even if I could transform into a dragon, even if we were remotely the same size...you know I can't beat him. He'll tear me out of the sky."

The vampire's eyes tightened and he quickly looked to the ground.

It was the exact thing he'd been chanting to himself since that fateful breakfast—the one where he'd stood in lone opposition to their plan. It was the exact same thing he'd been chanting for a long time before that, staring in silence at the ceiling, terrified for the girl sleeping by his side.

"We'll attack him as a wizard," he promised under his breath. "It won't come down to the two of you as dragons—I give you my word. But in the meantime?" He tilted his head coaxingly, trying to get her to smile. "I'd feel a lot better about our chances if you had this particular skill."

A ringing voice drifted up from the trees.

"As would the rest of us..."

They smiled again, then glanced towards the fae.

"How about I go and deal with him," Asher said reasonably, "and you can have a little time by yourself. Work on some of that quiet meditation you love so much."

She snorted in spite of herself. "I'd rank it right up with crocheting…"

The vampire pressed a kiss to her cheek, then headed off into the forest—leaving her standing by herself in the clearing, trying to imagine how it might feel to have wings.

Come on, she said to herself. *You can do this. It's literally in your blood.*

After casting a nervous glance over her shoulder she let her arms drift out to the side, closing her eyes and focusing on sensation instead of rational thoughts.

She didn't need to try to become a dragon. She already was a dragon. All she needed to do was figure out how to bring it to life…

…or suffer the prophetic consequences.

Her eyes flew open in a rage.

NO! No thinking! We decided no rational thoughts!

She closed them again with deliberate care.

Deprived of one sense, her others rushed to make up for it—painting as clear a picture as if she was using her eyes. The ground beneath her was soft and spongy, clinging to the soles of her shoes then retreating with a quiet hiss each time she leaned forward. A chilled breeze swept in from the north, whispering through the rain-soaked evergreens and filling the air with the sharp scent of pine. There was a family of tiny animals scurrying about thirty feet above her, chattering noisily as they scrambled over twisted knots of bark, and a pair of larks was splashing in the river, surfacing every now and again to pull berries from the stout branches of a nearby yew.

It was a game she used to play with her father—a man who could sweep gracefully through the forest without ever needing the luxury of his eyes.

She had put it to the test many times—riding on his shoulders with tiny hands clamped over his face. One time, when she was feeling very clever, she took out a scarf she'd stolen from her mother's chamber, wrapping it firmly around his face. He carried her as smoothly that day as any other, smiling to himself as she wondered out loud what kind of trickery must be at play.

Then one day, no different than the rest, he lifted her from his shoulders and set her in the grass. It was not a trick, he'd explained. It was a skill. One she must learn for herself.

Her childhood was full of those strange moments, when at the behest of her parents she was required to master some seemingly impossible task. One that appeared to have little bearing on her role as princess. Building a fire when left with nothing but damp wood, setting snares in the forest, navigating by the stars. Most often it was her father who taught her such things, but more often than not her mother came with them. Each lesson was to be taken as seriously as those prescribed by tutors in the schoolroom. Each was to carry the same weight.

It was the same way Ellanden had been riding a horse and shooting a bow since he was old enough to walk. The way he'd been made to travel every inch of ground governed by the Fae with his father—learning his kingdom, his people, his customs. Everyone from a common blacksmith to a priest. In the summer, he journeyed to the scorching desert and did the same with his mother.

In a similar vein, Asher had travelled to every library in the five kingdoms. He'd read books on philosophy and government before the others had mastered utensils. As such, he'd always been oddly eloquent for his age. He spoke in cadence, while the others used quick sentences. He never minced his words, but delivered fully-developed thoughts.

He had once caused an unintentional strike in the castle kitchens by delivering a lovely speech on the fundamental necessity of the arts.

Evie remembered like it was yesterday. He'd been standing on a crate of apples so as to be seen by those in the back of the room. When his governess came, she didn't have the heart to scold him.

So it shouldn't be impossible now, she thought, *to turn myself into a dragon.*

She could see with her eyes closed. She could howl at the moon and shoot waves of liquid fire from her hands. It should *not* be impossible to transform into a dragon.

And yet, somehow...it was.

She tried every technique both parents had taught her—the slow breathing, the even slower backwards counting, the ever-mocked meditation as she focused only on the soles of her feet.

In a particularly desperate moment, she attempted flapping.

This is never going to work.

She lowered her arms with a sigh, acknowledging the darker truth.

You don't want it to work.

Better to die on the ground, by a quick cut of the knife or a deadly spell, surrounded by her friends—people to catch her, and kiss her, and hold her when she died.

She had seen the beast. She remembered it well from her dreams.

She didn't want to die that way, with those thick talons tearing into her.

But I can't tell THEM anything like that...

Her ears perked up as two voices carried through the trees. They were hidden from sight, but not far—just over the crest of the little hills that stood at the base of the mountain.

With a mischievous smile she left the problem for another day and ghosted through the dense underbrush, moving with a skill and grace that would have made even her father proud. They were distracted—thank goodness. It was the only chance she ever stood at eavesdropping.

And from the sound of things, she wasn't the only one having problems.

"This is ridiculous," Ellanden cursed, throwing up his hands. "A waste of time."

The Prince of the Fae was as unaccustomed to the notion of failing as he was with the idea of spontaneously changing shape. It didn't help that the spectacle was being witnessed by one of his best friends. Or that it could technically be considered his magical birthright.

"I'm serious," he insisted, "this isn't going to happen. Let's go back."

Asher stared at him steadily, then shook his head. "You need to try—"

"I can't do it, all right!"

Rarely had the princess heard that note of defeat in his voice. It sounded out of place; cold and grim. He stood a moment longer, then suddenly walked away—turning towards the forest so the vampire could only hear him but not see the look on his face.

"All my life people, have been telling me to do this. All my life, no has ever questioned whether or not I actually can. This kind of magic...you have to *want* it for it to work. I don't."

Asher opened his mouth, but he spoke again quickly.

"I'm not the only one who thinks so." The words came out in a rush, but he was having trouble meeting the vampire's eyes. "Leonor told me once that such things aren't always passed down through a bloodline. Unless it's nurtured, magic tends to diminish or even fade."

The vampire laughed suddenly, and he lifted his eyes.

"Leonor would give his right arm if it meant he could drain every bit of Kreo magic from your blood. He's always been threatened by it—you know that. I'm not surprised at what he said."

"It doesn't mean he's wrong," the fae muttered, though his heart wasn't fully in it. "I mean, *look* at me, Ash. There's no question as to which side is dominant. Cosette's the same way. There's a chance she might never turn into a dragon. There's a chance I might never do this."

"Well...no," Asher said slowly, "not if that's—"

"I do not wish to speak of it!" Ellanden interrupted, afraid to let him finish. He strode away again, but kept circling back at the edge of the clearing—like a fish caught on a line. "All of those people back at the Kreo encampment, they recognized me as no prince. And why would they? We could not be more different, they and I. We could not be more incompatible."

The vampire let him rant himself out, listening with quiet patience. When he finally did speak, it was with that thoughtful deliberation that made others admire him so well.

"I think your mother's people are wild and frightful...and I adore them." He smiled to himself. "They have the biggest hearts. I think you think so, too."

It was very quiet for a moment.

"...well, you've always been exceptionally dim."

The vampire stepped closer, refusing to be put off. When his friend refused to look at him he stood calmly right in front, forcing him to meet those dark immortal eyes.

"I think you loved those people at the Kreo encampment," he said softly. "I think it kills you, what happened to them. And that you think on it, day and night."

It was quiet again, for a very long time, then the fae's shoulders fell with an open sigh.

"What does it matter?" he said, looking down at his hands. "If I still can't get it to work?"

The world in which they lived was so violent, so sudden, it was sometimes easy to forget those quiet moments one needed to breathe. Some doubts were as old as time, and just as hard to shake.

Asher took a step closer, clear sincerity in his eyes.

"You can do this," he said simply. "You were born to do it."

The princess watched through the trees as the effort began anew.

True to form, the fae's attempts were a great deal more composed than her own. The man couldn't shake that eternal poise if he tried. He was uncertain, though. An emotion as rare as that earlier despondency. As rare as defeat. It clung to him like a shadow he couldn't shake, closing his eyes and making that enchanting face tighten with just the hint of a frown.

You can do it...come on...

He didn't move much. Only someone with sharp eyes could have seen the way his arms had first trembled, then gone very still. The way his chin had tilted and his spine had stiffened—as if someone was drawing him skyward with an invisible string. His friends had very sharp eyes.

"You can do this," Asher chanted under his breath. "Come on."

It passed the point where Evie should have made herself known. She was on the verge of stepping out from behind the trees, when the fae let out a heavy sigh.

"Why must you always torment me? Nothing like this is ever asked of you."

Asher stepped back with a sudden grin, realizing only then he'd been holding his breath.

"Ellanden, I am asked every day *not* to end up eating you by the end." He moved another few steps away, shaking his head. "You talk about impossible requests..."

The fae looked at him coldly. "That was deliberately insensitive."

"Yes."

Ellanden glared a moment longer, then tried again. This time seemed almost vengeful—like he was trying to turn into a vampire himself. He gave up a moment later, panting and tired.

"Evie's going to laugh at you," Asher taunted, knowing full well it was more likely she was making daisy chains instead. "She's probably tapped into her own magic a dozen times by now."

"So we'll pretend that I have as well," the fae retorted, yawning. "Just walk up to her and say, *it worked—I'm Ellanden*, so I can to back to the fort and sleep." His eyes brightened with a sudden spark. "Then resist your every urge to get up her dress."

The vampire cuffed him with a grin, eyes flickering to the trees. "It isn't like that."

Ellanden raised his eyebrows with a wry look.

"*Really.*" It seemed impossible how one word could carry so much sarcasm. As if that wasn't enough, he tapped his ear. "I'm just across the square—"

"I mean, it isn't *always* like that," Asher interrupted, looking suddenly shy. "To be honest, it isn't how I expected...with the bond. I know in the beginning things are usually light and free, but nothing about this feels casual." He paused a moment, lips still parted. "There's a kind of weight to it. Something grounding, but...exactly the opposite. Does that make any sense?"

Ellanden stared at him for a long time. Then tilted his head with a coaxing smile.

"If I manage to shift into something else...will you stop talking about your feelings?"

The vampire froze in surprise, then looked rather dangerous. "How's Freya?"

The smile faded. "Screw off, Asher."

And that's my cue.

"Do I hear that winning team spirit?" Evie stepped forward with a grin, pleased to have startled them both. "Are you nearly finished? I tapped into my own magic a dozen times by now."

Asher flushed as she repeated his words, but Ellanden was merely grateful for the reprieve.

"Absolutely—let's head back," he replied, glancing around the clearing though there was nothing to gather. Perhaps something had been lost instead. "I didn't," he added suddenly, shooting her a sideways glance. "I didn't tap into anything."

She paused mid-step, thrown by his honesty.

"Oh...that's all right." Her cheeks flushed with guilt. "I was only joking. I didn't either."

He flashed a tight smile, then clapped her on the shoulder. "No one expected you to."

THE SUN WAS ALREADY dangling low in the sky by the time Evie and the others got back to the fort. Like a piece of low-hanging fruit, over-ripe and ready to be plucked. She stared at it a bit longer than was probably wise, then blinked as she made her way across the drawbridge. The heavy gate swung open and the three friends came to an abrupt stop. She blinked again.

At a glance, there was nothing unusual about the scene. The pack had awoken, the day had begun, and the courtyard was busy with the sounds of people going about their daily chores.

Mothers were wrangling children. Babies were screaming petulantly until someone took the time to make them smile. Young men were pointing vaguely in the direction of the forest, speaking to each other in quick, excited voices about which trails they would take that day to hunt.

She almost didn't notice the fae and the wolf kissing on the balcony.

Her feet stopped moving with the others as she stared up in surprise. They clearly weren't expected. Otherwise there was no way the little princess would have been anything but shy.

She looked happy now—perched lightly upon the railing with her fingertips resting on Seth's face. His arms circled around her with a tenderness apparent even from the other side of the busy square, keeping her balanced as his head bowed to hers with a little smile.

To be honest, it was a lovely picture. One that came to an abrupt end.

"*Cosette.*"

Ellanden's voice scorched the air between them, and even though he hadn't spoken very loud she leapt away as though she'd been burned. For a split second, those dark eyes swept over the fortress before coming to rest upon her cousin. The second after, she had vanished from sight.

Asher sighed quietly, hands in his pockets. "Was that really necessary?"

The prince's face was cold and remote. "If you want to be useful, Asher, why don't you busy yourself in the kitchen? Perhaps your girlfriend would like another piece of charred toast." He took another step forward, then flinched and glanced down at his chest. "I need to redress this wound. I'll speak to you both at dinner."

Such sharp departures weren't rare for the fae, especially when his mood had spoiled, and the others paid him no mind—rolling their eyes and taking each other's hands as they headed to the courtyard to the stairwell. Perhaps they wouldn't have done so if they'd seen the look on Seth's face.

Perhaps they would have done something to stop what happened next.

The shifter was still standing at the balcony, peering over the railing with an expression that made whoever caught sight of him hurry from the courtyard to do work elsewhere. He was the only one who hadn't shaken the confrontation; in fact, he seemed rather keen that it should continue.

He didn't bother with the stairs. He leapt straight over the edge.

"What the hell is your problem?!"

Before Ellanden could even lift his head the shifter planted two hands on his chest, shoving him halfway across the slick stone. He let out a breath of pain and surprise, one hand drifting to his tunic. But almost immediately, the shifter was shoving him again. Harder this time.

"What is your problem with me?" he demanded again. "Tell me it isn't the obvious, that I grew up in a village and she hails from a palace. Is it really something so bloody cynical—"

"Enough!" Ellanden caught his wrists before they could touch him again, throwing them back in the shifter's face. They stood closely for a moment, then he turned abruptly on his heel and headed towards the stairs. "I'm not speaking with you about this—"

"You're going to have to." Seth caught him by the arm, yanking him back. Never had he been so bold, but never had he been so angry. "Because this doesn't include you, Ellanden. That moment didn't include you. So if you have a problem with my peasant blood, you'll have to—"

"You foolish boy!" the fae cried, finally losing his temper. "Do you think I care about any of that? The two of us have stood side by side in battle. Your mother welcomed me to her table. You saved my cousin's life. Do you honestly think I care if you're poor—"

"Then what is it?" Seth shouted, refusing to back down. "Tell me what it is!"

The rest of the courtyard had basically emptied, only Evie and Asher remained frozen on the stairs. Somewhere above them, a door had opened. Two pairs of bright eyes were looking out.

Ellanden froze with lips parted, like someone had taken the words right out of his mouth. A flash of anger glinted in his eyes, a flash of pride. But he held himself back and kept silent.

The shifter stood there, waiting, then shook his head in disgust.

"You can't," he spat. "Because there's nothing to say. There's no earthly reason why the two of us shouldn't be together. This is jealousy, arrogance, and pride. Nothing else."

Again, the prince's eyes flashed with anger. But he offered only a curt nod. "Believe what you like. I'm going upstairs—"

"*Coward.*"

The word hissed between them like a snake, leaving one and striking the other. The princess and vampire tensed at the same time as Ellanden paused, his eyes still on the stairs.

There were some words a prince could not forgive. No matter how strong his resolve.

"You are a coward," Seth said again, taking a step closer, his eyes trained on the back of the fae's head. "All this time I thought you were simply protective, or perhaps you were guilty. After all, she was just a young girl when you *left*."

The fae went unnaturally still.

"That's right," Seth drew even closer, a wolf on the hunt, "you left. And it shattered her. It nearly broke her. The same way your parents left and it shattered the realm."

Evie's mouth fell open in shock.

Did he really feel this way? There was such venom in his voice.

Ellanden whirled around, incensed into action. Despite his own injury and the shifter's skill, he knocked him back with a violent burst of speed—almost growling himself.

"Don't talk about my family," he warned. "You know *nothing* about my family."

The shifter recovered his balance quickly, lifting his chin.

"I know they left when we needed them and you left Cosette the same way. I know that family is everything to a fae, but you abandoned a little girl, tear-stained and alone—"

There was a terrible cry as Ellanden flew towards him, another as the men collided sharply in the center of the courtyard, tussling a moment on the slick stones.

Asher moved to stop them, but Evie grabbed his sleeve.

This fight had been a long time coming. They would do nothing to hold it back.

"Enough!" Ellanden cried again, looking uncharacteristically disheveled as he strode away from the shifter, a hand raised in the air between them. "I have no wish to fight you!"

"Only to deny me a lifetime of happiness," Seth answered evenly. "Only to sabotage the happiness of your beloved cousin, for nothing more than a selfish whim."

"You know that isn't true," Ellanden insisted, unaware that the girl in question was watching from above with wide, unblinking eyes. "I would never—"

"Then what is your disagreement?" Seth swept abruptly towards him, closing the space. The anger was gone, replaced with a kind of breathless desperation—so manic and frustrated he didn't realize his fingers were clenched upon the fae's chest. "Tell me so I can fix it! Tell me so I can—"

"You're MORTAL, Seth!"

The shifter released him with a look of astonishment as that final piece fell into place. His lips parted, but there wasn't a sound in the courtyard—the entire place eerily quiet and still.

Only, the fae would not let it remain.

"Why must I be the one to say it?!" he cried. "Why must I be the only person here who doesn't pretend they don't know exactly what that means?!"

Evie slipped her hand into Asher's, a silent tear falling down her face.

Seth was at a loss, armed with nothing but the truth.

"...but I love her."

Ellanden made a harsh sound, somewhere between laughter and scorn.

"You love her," he repeated. "I have no doubt that you do. And I have no doubt that she loves you in return." His eyes burned with a simmering fire. "You are not the first. I have known other mortals who gave their hearts to those of immortal blood. Do you know what happened?"

The princess cringed at the tone of his voice, just as Seth did.

"You're right," he said shakily. "We shouldn't speak of it—"

"They died," Ellanden said simply. "They spent a few blissful decades, living that love to the fullest...and then they died." His voice grew abruptly quiet. "Do you know what happened then?"

The shifter could hardly look at him now. His eyes were shining and his face was pale as a sheet. Twice, he tried to walk away. But something held him back.

"The story continues, but there is only one person left to tell it. A person so ravaged and inconsolable with grief, they can hardly be counted as a person at all. Three years, I think, is the longest any of them have chosen to live. It is impossible to do otherwise, to live without the object of such undying devotion. The only answer is death. It is a path that most choose gladly."

He stepped closer, and for the first time his face showed a trace of pity. A softness that crept into his voice the longer he stared at the shifter's face.

"Your love is not a blessing to her, it is a curse that will leave her torn open and alone long after you've gone away. It gives me no joy to say it. You are a good man. You are simply blind."

One of the first memories Evie had with Ellanden they were about six years old, arguing over the rightful owner of a toy pony. Ironically enough, it was the same childhood token he had later passed on to Cosette. It had been hers originally, given to her as a charm by one of her father's many artisans. But you'd never know that, speaking to the fae. There was something so convincing about his words, so eloquent and earnest about the delivery, she ended up giving it to him freely.

He hadn't lost that innate persuasiveness; if anything, it had only sharpened as the years progressed. She'd learned to see past it. The problem was that he was usually right.

Evie didn't know if he was right now. But nothing he'd said was wrong.

Seth didn't know, either. His eyes flashed blindly to a room in the upper corridor. The anger that had guided him suddenly vanished, leaving him shaken and cold.

"It cannot be dismissed so easily," he stammered, "this feeling. I...I'm not going anywhere."

The fae leveled him with a look Evie knew very well. A look that made her feel unforgivably young. He let out a tired breath, hoping to have avoided this conversation altogether.

"And what is your plan?" he asked quietly. "Because I'm not sure what they teach in the village schools, but immortality means forever. She will love you forever, if you let her. But you'll only be there for a little while. And as long as the heavens are open, she'll remain alone."

The shifter's face split with indecision, torn between striking down an enemy and needing the counsel of a friend. He settled somewhere in the middle, almost pleading when he spoke.

"But it cannot be wrong," he whispered. "Such a thing...such a thing cannot be wrong."

"I'm not saying it's wrong," Ellanden said quietly. "I watched you stand in front of a horde of vampires if only to prolong her life—such a thing could never be wrong. But that doesn't mean there is hope in it, either. You must be strong. You must be strong so it does not crush you both."

For a moment, the shifter hung on his every word. Then he stalked away in sudden anger. "That's easy for you to say. An immortal prince, with the world at his calling. You are no prophet, Ellanden. You cannot say how such a thing will end—"

"No, and I do not claim to," the prince said angrily. "Only that it *will* end. It is a fate you cannot hope to change. One that will claim her life as surely as it takes your own."

When the shifter said nothing, that anger flared into something more.

"Why do you think I can't be with Freya?" he demanded. "When she is the *only* person in the entire world that I want. Why do you think I keep us at a distance, torturing myself day after day?"

The fae princess wasn't the only one listening on the balcony that day. Another pair of eyes was bright beside her—green, and so full of feeling it seemed as though they might burst apart.

She inched closer, holding all breath.

"I left her once, crying and alone. I'm not going to do that again."

In this, at least, Seth was able to rally.

"But that's not your decision. She can decide what she wants—"

"Freya waited ten years with my picture hanging on her wall," Ellanden interrupted, looking like it was physically paining him to speak. "Freya doesn't leave people. And if she wouldn't leave me?" He shook his head slowly, eyes haunted and grave. "That would destroy her."

A pair of tears slipped down the witch's face. She backed into shadow.

"But it *can* work," Seth insisted. "It's worked before. Your own parents—"

"My parents," Ellanden interrupted with a dry smile. "My mother tried to leave my father, did you know that? When she found out she was pregnant, she tried to give him a fairy potion to make him forget. Why? Because it *doesn't* work. It only worked because of the crown."

The shifter could think of nothing to say to this, but the fae had plenty.

"Why do you think I only take immortal girls to my bed?" he challenged. "Nymphs, naiads, fae. Do you think Freya would want to stay with me when she was forty, when she was fifty...and I was sixteen years old? Do you think it would be a happy life, hers and mine? Or one of longing? A fleeting passion, the loss of which would drown out whatever was to come?"

He stepped closer, willing the shifter to see things his way.

"It is because I love her that I would never subject her to such misery. You think I'm being unfair to you and Cosette? I cannot imagine how you could *possibly* be willing to do such a thing."

Seth shook his head, feeling almost light-headed. "But the crown...it could work again."

The fae sighed, having longed for such a thing many times himself. "They gave up the crown. And I don't know if this was made clear to you, peasant, but we're after a *dark* stone. I hardly think it would do the same thing, even if we weren't bound to destroy it."

A ringing silence fell over the courtyard, like someone had dropped an invisible anvil onto the ground. Its silent echoes rippled between them. Keeping them silent, keeping them still.

"All this time," Seth murmured, "I thought you hated me. When you saved my life in the grasslands...I truly didn't understand why."

Ellanden's gaze held steady a moment, then he shook his head.

"I don't hate you, I never could. You saved her life. I told you before, you will never have anything but my eternal gratitude." He paused slightly, gentling his tone. "But you're drawing her into something that is at best short-sighted. And at worst, eternally cruel."

There was a fleeting pause.

"I love her," Seth answered helplessly.

The fae nodded, then walked wearily to the stairs. He paused and sighed, his shoulders drooping. "Try not to. What do you think I've been doing this entire time..."

Chapter 11

The morning came too quickly. Evie woke in the gentle curve of the vampire's arms. For what felt like a long time she lay there in silence, breathing slowly, staring at the adjacent wall.

They had eaten their dinner quickly and gone to sleep without discussing what they'd overheard in the courtyard. They'd kissed each other in silence and flashed quick smiles before climbing under the covers, determined not to think about the fae's dark words.

But she couldn't help it. They'd seeped in.

She and Asher never had to worry about the prospect of immortality. While only one of them was technically blessed, the other had lucked into equal protection. As long as her mother wore the fated crown, she would be as her parents were themselves. Never to age, never to die.

Even after having learned they'd given it up, the hope was enough to sustain her. They would find their parents when this dreadful nightmare came to an end. They would journey to the enchanted house, reveal themselves to be alive, then everything would continue as it used to.

Their parents would return to the realm. There would be *five* kingdoms, not four. Her mother would take up the crown, the people would rejoice, and she would have eternity once again.

Unless the prophecy has its say...

They had discussed it and hidden from it. They had ignored it, minimalized it, and pretended it didn't matter—loudly proclaiming their indifference while moving on to lighter things.

But the fact remained...at least one of them was going to die.

She didn't know how to talk about it. She didn't know how to ignore it. Just when she'd managed to push it from her mind, the fae's words rang fresh in her ears.

It might not be a matter of mortality, but the question was the same.

How could she live without Asher? How could he live without her?

The vampire blinked open his eyes, as if he could hear his name.

"What's the matter?" he said sleepily. "What's wrong?"

She stiffened before she could stop it, then forced a sweet smile—stroking the side of his face. "Nothing, I was just...just thinking about what might happen today."

Even half-asleep, he managed to smile.

"My guess is another ogre. Like your grandmother, this one will paint."

She laughed before she could stop it, stroking back his dark hair.

He leaned into it without thinking, the curve of his forehead in the palm of her hand. A look of peaceful contentment drifted over him, but for once it didn't extend so far as herself.

"Asher?"

His eyes were shut again, but he was still awake. "Hmm?"

"Do you think we might go out walking today—just the two of us?" she asked with a touch of innocence. "And maybe later we could go back to the bell tower, fall sleep under the stars—"

"I'm not going to let anything happen to you."

She looked up suddenly to see him staring right at her, straight as an arrow, calm as his father had taught him to be. Those dark eyes found her, soothing the uneven breaths.

"That's not what I'm worried about," she whispered.

He stared at her a moment, then let out a quiet sigh. "You're worried about me," he said softly, sitting up on the mattress. "Because you think it's worse to be left behind. Because you're worried about what I might do…because of the bond."

Yes, exactly.

"No, nothing like that." She stared down at her hands, wondering how to phrase it. "Do you think Ellanden had a point yesterday with Seth? Do you think he was right in what he said?"

Asher sat up a little straighter, the blanket falling around his waist. "I don't think he was wrong," he said carefully. "In all our old stories, there's nothing more tragic than when a mortal and immortal fall in love. He's protective of Cosette. He's wracked with guilt about leaving and doesn't want to see it happen to her again. None of that is wrong."

He leaned down to catch her eye, waves of rippling onyx around his face.

"But none of that matters."

She shook her head suddenly, thrown off course.

"What does that mean?" she asked. "How could it not—"

"They're in love," he said simply. "You can't protect someone from falling in love. Ellanden speaks as though one must make a choice, but love isn't a willful decision. It's a matter of the heart."

Such things might have felt artificial coming from any other person, but each word sounded like poetry falling from his mouth. The princess stared for a moment, transfixed, then shook herself back to reality. One of the many hazards of waking up beside a vampire. You must keep your head.

"You should put your clothes on," she muttered. "You should wear clothes at all times."

He chuckled quietly, picking his pants up off the floor.

"At any rate, one must never listen to Ellanden about such things. The man has never felt the way he does for Freya. It terrifies him. The question of eternity is a perfect escape."

She grinned, watching as he slid the fabric over his legs.

"Oh yeah?" She arched an eyebrow, prying for more. "Is that what you two were talking about in the woods? All those pesky little feelings?"

He laughed again, remembering the way his insufferable friend had tried to exchange the promise of corporeal transformation just to avoid such a thing.

"Then we braided each other's hair."

She scooted closer on the bed, easing the shirt from his hands and dropping it back to the floor. He glanced down with a smile, but her eyes were serious.

"Did you mean what you said?" she asked softly. "That there's a weight to such a thing?"

Many times she'd tried to put words to the bond herself, but never had she summarized it so succinctly as her eloquent boyfriend. Something both grounding and freeing at the same time.

His face lit with a tender smile as he pressed her hand to his heart. "You no longer need to ask me. You know exactly how I feel."

She kissed him without thinking, then pulled back with a smile. Beneath her palm, his pulse quickened. Her fingers stretched over it, tapping lightly in time with the sound.

"I can't believe I never felt this before," she murmured, pressing her ear to it instead. "All those years I was trying...I wonder what changed."

He bit his lip, holding back a smile. "Yeah, I wonder what changed."

Her head snapped up. "Are you making fun of me?"

He shook his head quickly, those innocent eyes taking up half his face. It was a look that could have melted even the coldest of hearts. She stared a moment, then smacked him with a pillow.

"You absolutely are—you little bugger!" She lifted herself suddenly, anchoring her legs on both sides of him and raising the pillow. "Explain or die."

He shifted slightly, wrapping his fingers around her calves.

"You going to beat me to death with goose feathers?" he asked with a grin. "Everly, that could take years. At least slide a rock in there—"

"I'll smother you," she said simply, and proceeded to try.

Soon after coming to fully understand the phrase 'vampiric strength', she had delighted in testing those limits. Throwing herself with wild abandon against those arms like a child battling a statue, breathless with laughter, hopelessly outmatched, until she finally tired herself out.

"That was a *very* good try," he promised, pressing a kiss to her hair. "I almost moved."

Her eyes closed with exhaustion as she curled into a ball on his chest. "One day I'll destroy you..."

He laughed again, making little adjustments until the two of them were lying comfortably against the headboard, smiles lingering on their faces, both lost in thought.

"It was you," he said suddenly, arms circled around her back. "I know you've always tried, but that's why you can feel it now. Something...something changed because of you."

She looked up in surprise, wondering if he was telling the truth.

The myth was that vampires didn't have a heartbeat. But it was the kind of myth one took with a grain of salt. The reality was that no one had ever ventured close enough to find out.

At least, no one who had come back alive.

But it wasn't the same with Asher. She'd been pressing her fingers to his wrist since they were just children, determined to find the answer for herself. No matter how many times she was disappointed, she never continued to hope.

Then that day with the leopards, she felt it for herself.

"Something changed?" she repeated, hitching herself onto an elbow.

It was possible he flushed, glancing down so dark hair swept into his eyes.

"I don't really understand it myself. My father once said—" He caught himself quickly, then shook his head—staring at her once more. "All I know for certain is that it started with you."

THE COUPLE STAYED IN bed for a while longer, testing the limits of that bond themselves. Then they went downstairs for breakfast and conscripted the fae into another morning of magic practice.

"I thought we decided this was unnecessary." Ellanden glanced at the angry clouds swirling above them as he was forcibly marched across the drawbridge. "I thought we decided, because of my unparalleled talent on the battlefield, there was no need to develop further skills."

Evie snorted with laugher as Asher tightened his grip.

"And here I thought you'd be relieved to escape the fortress," he said lightly.

The fae shot him a quick look as they made their way into the trees. "You look unwell."

Asher touched his face in surprise. "I fed this morning—"

"Just in general."

The boys were still fighting amongst themselves when they reached the clearing the princess had been aiming for, and she suddenly turned around. Normally she would have either picked a side or interceded by now, but for the day's purposes it happened to be exactly what she needed.

"Go on then," she gestured between them, "take a swing."

They looked up in surprise, noticing for the first time that they'd stopped. It was the same pine grove where she'd practiced before. Only today, she was determined to see results.

"*Hit* him," Ellanden repeated, giving the vampire an appraising glance. "Like in the face?"

Asher stepped quickly away from him, moving forward with a frown. "What are you talking about?"

Evie squared her shoulders, testing her stance. "You told me yesterday I needed to find a way to make the pressure more immediate, more personal. The only time I tapped into magic before was when both your lives were at stake."

Asher nodded slowly, trying to follow along, then froze in surprise. "And...you want to repeat that experiment?"

Ellanden smiled behind him, while Evie nodded soundly.

"Absolutely."

The vampire blinked. "You must be joking."

"Makes perfect sense." Ellanden pulled a sword without hesitation, twirling it between his fingers as he strode forward. "En garde, Ash." The blade sliced the air above his head, making his dark hair fly backwards. "Keep in mind, Everly. The only way to stop me is as a *dragon*."

The fae gave her a playful wink, then attacked once more.

And so it begins...

For the next two hours, the friends engaged in a bizarre role-playing experiment. Ellanden would stretch the limits of his imagination for ways to murder the vampire, and Asher would repeatedly counter—sneaking up behind him, ready to sink his fangs into the prince's neck.

All the while, Evie would stand on the sidelines—trying her very best to shift.

The image alone was supposed to do it. While it might have been nothing more than a glorified sparring session, each man fought with enough skill to make it a terrifying sight to behold.

But they were having too much fun. And she was having too much fun watching.

"Okay—that's enough!"

Ellanden reached behind him for the vampire's hair, pushing him away and cringing in spite of himself. Given their history the fae was deeply unsettled by the 'I'm going to pretend to bite you' games, but he'd never admit such a thing, and the visual was arguably the most effective.

"I'm sorry, sweetheart," Asher teased, fangs bared. "Was that a little too intense?"

Ellanden shoved him away, rubbing the side of his neck.

"You need to yank his head back a little more," Evie called from the log upon which she'd perched. "Make it realistic."

Asher nodded with a grin.

"Like this—"

The tip of a blade appeared at his throat, tilting up his chin.

"More like *this*, Asher."

The vampire grinned, knocking it away with a swat of his hand.

While the princess had essentially given up and was enjoying the scene as a spectator sport, the men had utterly exhausted themselves with the effort of attacking such a difficult opponent for such a sustained period of time. The good thing about such fights is that they are usually over quickly. One didn't charge the same person again and again and again.

"Is this helping you?" Asher called, trying to force his way out of a headlock while the fae secretly cut his hair. "You tapping into those famous protective instincts? Getting any scales?"

"Absolutely, babe—this is totally helping!"

"*Everly.*"

"You just hang in there!"

The men glanced at each other in silence. A lock of dark hair fell to the ground.

"I don't think she's taking this seriously," Ellanden offered.

"...did you just cut my hair?"

The fighting began anew as the princess glanced up at the fortress, glimpsing the point of the bell tower through the trees. A blanket of angry-looking clouds was settling around it. The air was damp and crackled with electric energy, the precursor to a springtime storm.

"We should get some snacks," she murmured.

A pinecone hit the side of her face.

"How's the whole *dragon* thing coming?" Ellanden called testily, dropping suddenly to the forest floor when the vampire kicked out his knees. "You know—the magical transformation?"

"I did it already—you missed it." She stretched onto her back, hair dangling over the log. "I was impossibly ferocious." Her hands curled into the air. "These giant golden claws..."

The men shared another look. A second later, they were upon her.

"Hey!" she shrieked as she was pulled off the tree. She hit the ground with a dull thud, then straightened up to see a pair of imposing men staring down at her. Arms crossed, faces stern. The anger vanished in a blink. "I mean...you guys have done a really good job. Such *warriors*, my men."

Ellanden rolled his eyes, while Asher smiled in spite of himself.

"Don't get discouraged," he said gently. There were leaves in his hair and a gash running up the side of his face, but his eyes were only for the princess. "It's going to take some time. It took your mother some time. She literally jumped off a cliff just to make it happen."

A terrifying silence fell between them, and the vampire paled in sudden panic.

"I didn't mean—"

"You should *absolutely* jump off a cliff," Ellanden interrupted excitedly.

"I should *totally* jump off a cliff," Evie agreed at once, twisting around to see how close they were to the peak of the mountain. "I wonder if it would actually—"

"*Stop it!*"

Asher raised his voice, stepping between them. One hand spun Evie back around as the other smacked Ellanden upside the head. It wasn't the first time he'd been forced to separate them.

"You are *terrible* influences on each other," he muttered. "It's a miracle either of you managed to survive this long."

There was a guilty pause, followed by the signature deflection.

"You were the one who suggested it, Asher."

"You were the one who mentioned the cliff."

The vampire pursed his lips, counting out silent breaths.

"How about we head inside for a break," he suggested patiently. "The two of you can get some food. I can punch a pillow while imagining your faces. We can all meet back here after the—"

The skies opened above them.

"—storm."

There was no time to take cover. There was no time to make it back to the fort. With a shout of surprise, the three friends dove under the nearest outcropping—staring in silence as what felt like all the water in the five kingdoms came down upon their heads.

Perfect, just perfect. Evie held out a tentative hand, then retracted it at once. *Just when I figured out the key to my transformation. The cliff is probably too slippery now...*

"We could make a run for the drawbridge," Ellanden offered half-heartedly. As he spoke, a flash of lightning split the sky in two. "...or not."

With a trio of sighs, the friends settled back to wait.

As if the torrential downpour wasn't enough, the temperature had dropped sharply as a bitter wind swept down from the north. They might be in the early weeks of spring, but a lingering winter was still upon them. The ground was soon slick with chilled mud, seeping into their clothes.

The rest of them are probably still sleeping at the fortress, the princess thought miserably, shaking out the skirt of her dress. *Should never have gotten out of bed—*

The sound of quiet laughter interrupted her thoughts.

She and Ellanden turned incredulously to Asher. His head was bowed and his shoulders were silently shaking. When he felt their eyes he tried to control himself, but to no avail.

"What is it?" Evie demanded.

He shook his head quickly.

"Tell us," Ellanden insisted. "What could you *possibly* find funny right now?"

The vampire looked affectionately at the fae.

"Do you remember that picnic in Taviel? That summer when we were kids?"

Ellanden's face softened into a sudden smile.

"And it started raining?" he asked. Asher laughed again. "You asked me to command the rain to stop. Since one of the guards had just told you I was a prince."

"You assured me you could do it."

Evie grinned, remembering as well. "You spent the rest of the afternoon trying," she recalled, picturing those little fists shaking at the sky. "And then your Aunt Serafina came to find us and actually *did* command the rain to stop."

The conversation came to a pause, then Ellanden shrugged it off.

"Yeah, well...she's always been a showoff."

They fell silent again, staring out at the rain.

Instead of lightening up, as these sudden storms were known to do, the rains were getting worse. A steady stream of water was coming down the mountain, pooling around their feet.

A few long minutes passed, then Ellanden let out a quiet sigh.

"I can't change the weather, Ash."

The vampire threw him a quick glance, then turned back to the trees. "Maybe," he conceded. "But I can't think of a better time to try."

The challenge was soft-spoken but too direct to ignore, punctuated by the constant splash of water. The fae stilled self-consciously, then his eyes drifted tentatively up to the sky.

It was the domain of his people, the natural elements, entrusted to them for safekeeping by those powers that drifted among the stars. Their influence varied. Not many Fae could actually shape the weather, but the gift ran in his family, hovering just a few hundred years out of reach.

Without seeming to think his hands lifted, then he lowered them quickly to his sides. A flush of embarrassment colored his cheeks and he stepped back as far as the rocks would allow.

"I think Evie would have an easier time turning into a dragon."

She elbowed him in the ribs. "*Hey.*"

Asher merely shrugged, still staring up at the sky. "It was just a passing thought. We can wait out the storm."

For the next little while, that's exactly what they did—standing in silence as torrents of water poured down the side of the mountain, watching as the overhanging branches bowed beneath it, dipping ever lower on the trees. Claps of thunder rumbled the ground beneath them and the lightning was almost directly over them, painting their skin in eerie shades every time it flashed.

There was something almost hypnotic about it. Time ceased to matter and Evie found herself staring in a kind of trance, jumping in surprise when Asher spoke suddenly beside her.

"Ellanden."

A strange look came over the fae as he stepped out from beneath the rocks, gliding into the clearing in a kind of suspension, as if propelled by forces they weren't able to see. The rain soaked him quickly, drenching his clothes and painting his hair to the sides of his face, but he was oddly indifferent to it. The storm did not concern him. The only thing that mattered was the sky.

What in seven hells is he doing?

Evie stepped closer to Asher, squinting out into the rain.

He came to a stop in the middle of the clearing, tilting his face to the clouds. A thousand tons of water came down on his head, but he stared upwards with a look of perfect calm as if he was waiting for something—the answer to a question that had not yet been revealed.

Then all at once...it happened.

It started small, just a tiny glimmer—as if both the day and the storm had yielded suddenly to give way to the light of the moon. Before the princess' eyes could adjust it suddenly expanded, shimmering around Ellanden like a celestial halo, painting his outline in the same white-silver glow.

He bowed his head slightly, getting used to the feeling.

It came slowly at first then swept over him quickly, blossoming like a drop of warmth beneath his skin. Before long, his entire body was flushed with it—lighting him with the same breathtaking animation that his friends saw only on rare occasions—in the heat of battle, or in the arms of his mother, or when he'd been told a particularly good joke.

He smiled ever so slightly, his eyes shining like a beacon. Then with an ease that confounded the chaos around him, both arms drifted into the air. It was like parting a curtain, so simple and so fast. Beneath the invisible grip of his fingers, the rain around them suddenly ceased to fall.

"I can't believe it," Asher breathed, eyes wide with wonder as he and the princess stepped slowly out from beneath the rocks.

The ground around them was still flooded, thick with the water pouring down from the mountains, but the sky above was calm and clear. Unless Evie's eyes were fooling her, she could have sworn she saw the faintest hint of the sun.

It was a miracle, plain and simple. But their friend had high standards.

Miracles had never been enough.

With a look of deep concentration he closed his eyes, tilting back his head as that ethereal glow around him grew almost painfully bright. After a few seconds both the princess and the vampire had to turn their eyes, looking not at the fae himself but the new world he was creating.

That vicious springtime storm...was suddenly gone.

Evie stepped back instinctively, the way one might do at the sudden burst of a sunrise or the flash of a falling star. The dark clouds that had been chasing them all morning vanished like cobwebs swept away, replaced instead with a burning, blinding sun.

There was a small inhale of breath, like the sigh of someone just awoken, as the fae opened his eyes. He crossed himself with a gesture made by the elders of his people, then turned towards the others as that blinding glow faded into a breathtaking smile.

"Did you see?"

Evie almost laughed aloud.

No—we missed it!

With a strange kind of hesitation, she and Asher walked forward—seeing one of their oldest friends in a new and staggering light. He didn't look any different. Just the same as he always did. Only perhaps now they realized how different he'd always looked. That light never fully left him.

"We saw," Asher said cautiously, eyes sweeping over his skin. When at last they returned to his face, they danced with a twinkling smile. "I guess you're a prince after all."

Ellanden took a step closer, then slumped forward—falling into the arms of his friends.

"I'm all right," he murmured. as they clustered around him. "I'm just...very tired."

The princess gripped him tightly, half-expecting it to burn her hands.

"You're allowed," she replied, shivering involuntarily.

He found his balance slowly, taking deep and measured breaths. "Thank you," he said suddenly, turning to Asher, "for making me do that."

The vampire shook his head, unable to look away. "I didn't do anything—that was all you." He held back the obvious question and asked another instead. "Would you like to rest for a while? There's no need to—"

"No, let's go back to the fort." He glanced suddenly through the trees, looking far more like the impatient prince. "I'm starving."

You're allowed.

Together the three of them hiked slowly from the clearing, much more slowly than the fae was aware at the time. It wasn't until the last possible minute that he paused suddenly, casting a final look at the sky. A peculiar look swept over him, fading into the shadow of a frown.

"What is it?" Asher asked, following his gaze.

"I had thought..." He trailed off, shaking his head. "It's nothing."

Asher caught him with a curious smile. "Tell me."

The prince hesitated, then glanced up at the sky. "I had something of a dream of this. Years ago, when I was travelling with my mother. It was the same feeling. Streaks of broken light..." He flushed self-consciously. "I'd been bitten by a snake, so it was nothing but a fever dream."

Bitten by a snake?

The princess stared with wide eyes.

Like it was yesterday, she remembered the two of them sitting in the grass outside the vampire encampment, trading stories of their time with the Kreo chiefs. When she recounted her vision question, he'd admitted to having one as well.

You're lucky, you got to drink the venom, he'd said. *I had to let the snake bite me.*

Asher raised his eyebrows with a curious frown.

"You dreamt you were holding back the rain?"

Ellanden shook his head. "No, it was stranger. I was holding back the sky."

IT WAS A SLOW WALK the rest of the way back to the fort, but after the celestial display back in the forest none of the friends was in a particular hurry. They ambled along at a leisurely pace, watching the sunlight catch tiny droplets still hanging from the branches. Remembering to themselves with secret smiles.

Maybe the fates had done well to send him from the Kreo, back into the arms of the Fae, Evie thought as they wandered down the trail. *It was their magic he'd summoned. Not the desert people's.*

She glanced up at Ellanden, wondering if she should say as much. However, a branch snapped suddenly in the forest and the three of them came to an abrupt stop.

"Who's there?" Asher called warily, scanning with his bright eyes.

It was too deliberate a sound to have been made by accident, and too isolated to suggest a passing animal. Such things spoke to larger creatures—predators, hunters, slavers.

The kind of trouble they'd seen too often since striking out on their own.

A ringing silence followed his question, growing louder by the second. Acting on instinct the friends fanned out, each facing a separate direction. Asher's fangs cut slowly into his lower lip, Evie raised a hand of fire, and Ellanden's fingers twitched towards the handle of his blade.

There was another snap. Then another.

A second later, two people stepped casually into the sun.

"What the hell's the matter with you?" Evie demanded, extinguishing the flames in a fist of smoke. "Didn't you hear Asher call?"

Cosette shrugged innocently, Seth grinning beside her.

"The shifter wanted to see if the vampire would bare his fangs," she replied, much to the blushing dismay of her companion. "I told him it's not that interesting, all things considered."

Asher's eyes cooled as he retracted them with a hiss.

"Actually, we were just coming to find you," Cosette continued. "I figured you were out here practicing and got caught in the storm. But the weather cleared up." She glanced at the cloudless sky with a curious frown. "Strange, right?"

Evie's eyes flickered to Ellanden, but the prince merely nodded. "Strange."

And speaking of...

In a sudden flash of adolescence, she glanced between him and Seth—wondering if the dynamic had changed, wondering if there was a chance they might come to blows. Conversations didn't happen often, like the one they'd had in the courtyard. Blood had almost been spilled.

But the two men acted as if nothing had happened. Even more than that, Seth flashed what looked like a genuine smile. Granted, he was still holding tight to Cosette's hand.

Ellanden glanced between them, but didn't say a word.

"Any luck?" the shifter asked brightly, eyes resting on the princess.

Nope—not me.

She shook her head. "Not my day, I guess."

"We were heading back to get some lunch," Asher added casually. If his friend wasn't yet ready to share the secret, he would keep it as well. "But I'd be more than happy to stay out here and show Seth just how exciting these fangs can be..."

He trailed off just as the others heard it, just as reflexive shivers raced up their skin. It wasn't often that something so large could get so close. There was a reason for that.

Those were the instincts that kept you alive.

Evie turned slowly, heart pounding, the image pulsing behind her eyes. For as long as she'd wandered in the forest, she'd never heard that particular growl. It was the kind that haunted children in nightmares, that sent them screaming into their mother's arms.

There was nothing in the woods behind her, but that didn't take long to change. Almost the second the friends turned around, the ferns parted and a living monster stepped into the sun.

I don't believe it...that's a hellhound.

THE ONLY REACTION WAS shock. That was the only thing that made sense.

Shock that it was there. Shock that it was real. Shock that it was staring at them with those yellow eyes, debating the exact manner in which it wanted to kill them.

At this point, it wouldn't be hard.

The friends were frozen in place, all their skills forgotten. All the weapons going loose in their hands. How could you fight a nightmare? How could you not stand before it like a frightened child—hoping someone would come to save you, hoping it would simply go away?

Then it growled again, and they remembered how to move.

"A hellhound," Seth said faintly, backing a step away. "That's a hellhound, right? Like from old stories, and..."

And very, very bad dreams?

The others couldn't answer, but it was there all the same.

"A hellhound," Ellanden repeated, in a voice slightly higher than usual. He swallowed hard, then nodded. "No big deal. My father's killed countless hellhounds."

In a quiet panic, he glanced at Cosette for confirmation. The girl was backing away slowly, her eyes locked on the beast, but she still managed to nod.

"My father tended to befriend them, then fall into years of dark enchantment," she began nervously, "but afterwards—yes. He killed them as well."

"That's great," Seth muttered, silently comparing it against every creature he'd fought in the arena. He didn't like where it ended up. "So how do we kill it? Evie's fire?"

The princess lifted her hands slowly, but Asher lowered them back down.

"It's a short pounce away," he murmured, backing up with the rest of them. "Faster than the fire would take to reach it. It might burn...but it would get one of us as well. Better to distract it."

Distract it?

Evie's legs trembled as she pictured a massive ball.

"How should we do that?" she breathed.

Ellanden considered a moment. "Give it something it wants."

There was a beat of silence, then he nudged Seth forward.

Are you KIDDING me?!

The princess threw him a look of shock, but the fae was smiling. His own shock had worn away and that impulsive teenager was back, the one who'd recently bested a lightning storm.

"It's a glorified dog," he said boldly, drawing his blade. "We've fought worse than this. It bleeds like anything else." He waved the shifter forward. "After you, love."

Seth drew his own blade, took a faltering step, then froze.

"This is payback for the vampires, isn't it? When I offered you in Cosette's place?"

Ellanden merely smiled. "Do your little dog trick—it'll love it."

"Landi," Asher chided with strained patience.

"Maybe it'll think you're its idiot cousin."

"Ellanden."

"Relax," Ellanden stepped forward with a grin, "I'll kill it."

But the moment he lifted his blade, several things happened at once.

The hellhound growled, the ground trembled and that celestial fatigue washed over him like a drug, weighting the sword in his hand.

It clattered to the ground by his feet.

An impressive display.

The hound growled again and he stepped back, looking pale.

"On second thought...Asher, you kill it."

"Why is a hellhound even here?" Cosette asked shakily, gripping the small knife she'd happened to bring from the fort. "Things like this don't just—"

"*Hello?*"

A voice echoed in the distance, bringing their world to a sudden stop.

Despite her earlier reluctance, it seemed that Freya had decided to join them after all. She was paused on the edge of the drawbridge, staring out towards the trees. From such a distance, she couldn't see them. Neither could she see the beast, who'd just picked up her scent on the breeze.

It turned its head towards her, lips curled back in an anticipatory snarl.

Seven hells!

Ellanden was the first to move, jumping without thought right on top of the beast—anything to divert its attention from the lovely girl he'd sworn not to love. The creature twisted and roared, lifting a deadly paw to dislodge him, but then Asher was there—leaping straight over them both and tackling the fae to the ground. They landed in a pile in the ferns, sprawled and vulnerable. But before the hound could strike, Cosette and Seth appeared in front of them. Blunted knives and childhood fears made little difference now; their blood was high and they would fight the creature all the same.

...and they will lose.

Evie saw it playing out like something from a dream—each fleeting detail and micro-expression burning into the dark recesses of her brain.

The way Cosette let out a fearsome cry as Seth shifted on the spot. The way Asher seized Ellanden by the cloak, yanking him back to his feet. Even the distant girl on the drawbridge, staring curiously at the forest, wondering if she'd heard or merely imagined such a ferocious howl.

It's going to destroy them. They don't have the strength or weapons to fight it. This isn't some random predator, it's a hellhound. They need something bigger. They need something more.

Those were the last coherent thoughts that raced through her mind—that abstract desire, the overwhelming to be the answer to their problem, to be the thing that stood in its way.

That's when the princess vanished. And a fiery dragon rose up in her place.

Chapter 12

How did one explain it? The princess was at a loss. Because at some point, she had stopped being a princess. At some point, she became something else instead.

"So you didn't know what would happen?" Asher asked for the hundredth time.

The two were lying in bed together, having spent the entire day recovering from her sudden bursting into a creature of flames. It had happened just in the nick of time. While the rest of her friends were scattered and scarcely armed, easy targets, the hound had picked up on the scent of the witch.

Freya would have been torn to pieces if the princess hadn't managed the transformation exactly when she had. If that mighty dragon hadn't swooped out of the trees in a burst of fire and pulled the hellhound straight off the drawbridge in a wild snapping of its jaws.

Evie remembered each moment perfectly. The way her wings had felt like sails, cupping the wind and lifting her effortlessly into the sparkling sky. The way the beast had smelled foul, even from a distance. The way its bones had splintered and snapped inside her mouth. The two had blended together, and that's what she'd been thinking about the moment the creature had died.

Splinters and sails.

She remembered wishing she hadn't touched it, wishing that she had sprayed it with fire or scratched it with her claws instead. But such things hadn't occurred to her in the moment. Her only thought was for Freya. Her only thought was to get it off the bridge. She hadn't even noticed the screaming villagers until she'd ripped the beast to pieces and was peering down tentatively inside.

But that's not what Asher had asked.

"I didn't know," she said quietly, curling into him. "I only knew I had to stop it."

After coming down from the ocean of adrenaline racing through her veins, the princess was feeling unexpectedly subdued. Perhaps because, unlike the handsome vampire lying beside her, she had spent the day plagued with another question instead.

What was a hellhound doing in the forest?

They were agents of death, equipped with other-worldly senses and bred in pestilence and shadow in the darkest corners beyond the realm. In places like the Dunes, places where the friends were going, they would be plentiful enough. But here? Even amidst the chaos that had gripped the kingdoms since the departure of their parents, such creatures would be hard to find.

This one hadn't wandered into the woods by the fort by accident. It hadn't been wandering at all. It had been hunting. Even worse...it had been scouting.

"Evie?"

She lifted her head to see Asher watching her expectantly, his dark eyes glowing in the shadows. It was clear that he'd asked her something, but her head had been miles away.

"I'm sorry—what did you say?"

He stared a moment longer, then his face melted into a smile. Such pensive trances were usually his domain. The rest of them had an almost clinical inability to stop talking.

"It's not important," he said graciously, pulling her into his arms. The two of them nestled together as if they'd been doing it for years—her cheek resting on his chest, his chin resting in her hair. It was quiet for a while, then he smiled again. "Ellanden will be angry you've upstaged him."

She glanced up with surprise, then settled back with a grin. "You know what...I'm actually not sure if that's true."

While the fae could usually be counted on to boast of his many accomplishments, this one had struck him a different way. The entire rest of the day, he hadn't said a word to the others about what he'd done. In light of the dragon, it was easy to keep such news to himself. But he hadn't told them in the woods, either. Evie wasn't sure the thought had even crossed his mind.

"I couldn't have imagined that happening," she continued softly, rolling onto the vampire's chest. "It was like a painting. Like one of our stories from the nursery had suddenly come to life."

Asher nodded slowly, eyes widening as he remembered.

"I was giving him a hard time," he admitted. "Just getting him to try. His father didn't do such a thing for hundreds of years, and neither did Serafina. Ellanden is sixteen. I can't..." He shook his head incredulously, at a loss for words. "I don't even know what to say."

They lay there in silence, then Evie tentatively lifted her head.

"So what's *your* big trick, Asher?"

They glanced at each other, then burst out laughing.

It went on for a long time—turning into tickling, turning into kissing, turning back to laughing—before they settled down the way they'd been before. Smiles still lighting up their faces.

"Don't even joke," he grinned, running his thumbs up and down her arms. "At this point, I'll have to move some literal mountains if I want to pull my own weight in this group."

"Perhaps you could fetch water and food for the rest of us," she suggested casually. "Or you could just let me use you shamelessly for bed stuff."

His arms tightened with another grin.

"*That's* not a bad idea. Kind of leaves Landi out in the cold, though."

She rolled on top of him, lips fluttering in his ear. "People have fawned over Ellanden his whole life. A little rejection will be good for him..."

A FEW HOURS LATER ASHER was fast asleep, but the princess still lay awake beside him. Staring up at the ceiling, tracing mindless shapes against the wall.

That question refused to leave her. No matter how she tried to distract herself it kept coming back, like a tiny thorn wedged deep in her mind.

What was a hellhound doing in the forest?

She didn't plan on leaving. It wasn't until she was halfway to the door that she even realized she'd gotten out of bed. With a backwards glance at the sleeping vampire, she slipped a robe over her shoulders and ghosted silently into the hall.

Someone had the answer to her question. And she was guessing that person was still awake.

"Evie?" Adelaide pulled open her door in surprise, wearing a robe quite similar to the one the princess was wearing herself. The simple cotton gowns made in the village. "What's the matter?"

The princess shivered a little, bare feet pressed against the stone. "May I come inside?"

The door swung open immediately as her grandmother beckoned her into the room, pulling straight the blankets on the bed before gesturing her to sit down.

Her bright eyes swept over the young girl with silent concern. She'd been expecting this visit. She'd been waiting for it to happen since the moment that fiery dragon swooped across the sky.

The answer came before the question had even been asked.

"The beast answered to Kaleb," she said quietly. "When the house was destroyed, when the ogre was killed, when I left...he must have felt it. Even as a boy, he was highly attuned to such things. Once he grew into his power..." Her face tightened slowly as she stared the princess right in the eyes. "It will not be the last monster prowling in the night."

Silence fell between them, filling up every inch of the room.

The princess wasn't shocked by the news, nor was she particularly dismayed. It was the answer she'd been expecting, one that would forever shape the days to come.

"We can't stay here," she finally said.

Adelaide's eyes filled with tears as she shook her head. "No, my dear. You can't."

Evie lifted her gaze slowly. "But such a thing is impossible to fight alone."

She remembered how it felt when the dragon had taken hold. It was wild and strong and raw and...completely unpredictable. Such a thing could not yet be counted upon, and the time to master it had run out. It was a miracle she'd transformed when she did. Another fraction of a second, and one of her closest friends would be dead. The others would be forever broken with grief.

They couldn't keep counting on miracles. Not if they wanted to win this fight.

Perhaps they only needed one more.

ASHER WAS STILL ASLEEP when she burst back into their room, grabbing him by the wrist and pulling with all her might. His eyes snapped open and he fought back a hiss—staring in surprise.

"...good morning?"

"Not quite yet," she panted, still tugging on his arm. "But you need to get up. I had an idea."

His body resisted the notion, curving longingly towards the bed, but his girlfriend had just turned into a dragon and certain allowances had to be made.

Besides, it was a new relationship. Sleepless favors were not optional.

"I need to get dressed," he mumbled, pushing back his hair. In her excitement to drag him to the door, the princess had not yet noticed he was still naked. "Evie, hold on a second—"

A pair of pants hit him in the face.

"I'll time you."

Exactly three seconds later, they were hurrying down the outer corridor that squared along the edge of the courtyard—their bare feet splashing in the icy puddles on the stone. He hadn't yet asked where they were going. Most of his questions had been distractedly ignored. But he didn't seem surprised when they came to a sudden stop in front of a large oak door.

"Open it," she commanded.

He lifted a hand, then paused. "Can't we just knock—"

"*Now*, Ash. He'll be sleeping."

The vampire shot her a quick look, then wedged his fingers beneath the hinges—bending the metal until the screws that held them together came loose. With hardly a sound he lifted the door aside and stepped quickly through the frame, replacing it quickly once they were inside.

Ellanden was fast asleep, sprawled out across the entire length of the bed. He might have channeled some kind of starlit godling in the forest, but in the crushing fatigue that followed he had reverted to a sleep-starved adolescent—legs dangling over the side of the mattress, one arm thrown carelessly across his face.

He was also most assuredly naked beneath the covers.

The vampire thought of this. The princess did not.

"Why don't you let me wake him," Asher offered swiftly. "Just give him a minute to—"

But Evie was already moving across the room, lighting the candle beside his bed.

"Landi—wake up."

He stirred, but remained generally comatose—mumbling incoherently in his sleep.

"Wake up," she insisted, shaking him roughly. "I have a proposition for you."

His dark eyes blinked open slowly, wincing against the light of the flame. For a moment he merely stared at the princess, unsure whether he was still dreaming. Then his gaze drifted behind her to where the vampire was cowering apologetically, half-naked, by the door.

He blinked again, then frowned.

"Guys...that would be a *really* bad idea."

Asher banged his head against the wall, while Evie shook hers impatiently.

"I spoke with my grandmother about the hellhound and she confirmed my fears—it wasn't here randomly. It answered to Kaleb. And it's only the beginning of what's yet to come."

That woke them both.

"She said that?" Asher asked nervously, crossing to the bed. "She's sure?"

Evie nodded slowly, watching them both at the same time.

"I transformed into a dragon yesterday," she began carefully, "a dragon that can fly across great distances. A dragon that can cover hundreds of miles in the span of a day."

The boys stared back blankly.

"Yeah, I remember."

"Did you literally break in here just to boast?"

She pulled in a deep breath, waiting for it to click. "Instead of heading west...I think we should head east."

There was a beat of silence.

Ellanden's mouth fell open, while Asher froze in surprise.

"You're...you're sure?" Asher stammered.

She nodded again, keeping her eyes on them both.

"When our parents received their own prophecy, they wandered the woods as long as they had to. They learned what skills were required, battled whoever they must." She paused ever so slightly. "Then as *soon* as they were able, they assembled an army to march to the Dunes."

The light of the solitary candle danced between them, the reflection flickering in those wide eyes. But outside the window dawn was breaking, announcing the arrival of a new day.

"We can get to them now." Her voice was only a whisper. "We can get there if I fly. This isn't an enemy we can fight by ourselves; there can be no lasting peace if the realm is divided. It's time to put this part of the journey behind us. It's…it's time to go home."

***

THE NEWS WAS RECEIVED differently by the others. Cosette had seen her parents only a few months before, Seth knew them only from stories, and Freya was nowhere to be found.

"Where is she?" Ellanden asked softly. He had been unable to find the witch since the day before. Rather, he'd been actively prevented from seeing her by his formidable little cousin.

"She's packing," Cosette answered shortly. "Leave her alone."

…packing.

Evie glanced around the courtyard before her eyes drifted up to the sky.

Because this is really happening. Because we're really going to leave.

For the first time since deciding earlier that morning, the reality of what was about to happen settled in hard—stealing the breath right from her lungs.

I'm going to see my mother again. I'm going to see my father.

A pale sheen of panic washed over her face.

…what will they think of me?

Asher and Ellanden had frozen beside her, struck with the same terrifying thought.

They said nothing, of course. Each one nodded politely as Seth and Cosette separated away; each one glanced casually at the shifters, as though simply counting the time until they could depart.

Then, with a sudden compulsion, the vampire turned.

"You look older," he said, lifting a finger to the newly angled planes of the fae's face. "We all look a little older. That time spent in the cave...I wouldn't say we're sixteen."

Evie's fingers drifted to her cheeks.

How is it possible we don't know?

He was right, of course. She had thought the same thing many times—seeing it in the others, though she was unable to track such changes in herself.

The men had always been tall and athletic. *Strapping* was a word she'd heard thrown around the corridors and stairwells of the castle, whispered in hushed voices that vanished by the time she could turn around. But there had been something boyish to them as well.

Both were beautiful, but lacked the commanding presence of their parents. The swords at their sides hung like mere decorations, flawless and gleaming from lack of use.

But all that had changed in the forest.

They still had that freshness, caught in the eternal grip of a radiant youth, but the childish quality was gone. It had evened out to something a bit sharper, a bit older. Something a bit more clearly defined. Those royal hands were strong and callused. Though quick to smile, there was a steadiness to them now that spoke to the places they'd been since leaving the castle.

Like uncut stones left out to be smoothed by the wind and sun.

And what about me? Do I still appear the same?

Ellanden caught his breath, trying to control his racing heart.

"How much should we tell them?" he asked quietly, eyes drifting over the stone walls to the eastern sky. "So much has happened...what if they cannot forgive?"

Evie followed his gaze, wondering the same thing.

"We will tell them everything," Asher finally answered, quiet but calm. "And they will forgive it. They are our parents—they will always forgive."

...tell that to Kaleb.

"What are we talking about?" Seth chimed back into the conversation, turning from the Fae princess with a smile still lingering on his face. "My grand introduction to royalty, I hope."

Evie grinned in spite of herself.

"How many times must I say it—*we're* royalty. You've already met us."

He shook his head patiently. "That's not the same thing."

"Actually, I wasn't sure you were coming with us," Ellanden said softly, looking him up and down. "Of course you're more than welcome, but I didn't know what you'd decide."

"What do you mean?" Cosette asked in alarm. "Why wouldn't he be coming with us?"

For once, the prince didn't antagonize her. He answered with a quiet calm.

"Because this isn't his fight. Because he's known us a few weeks. Because he's finally back home. And it's not like..." He glanced around the fort. "This place needs someone like him."

The retort died on Cosette's lips as she turned to the shifter instead. Always so steady, those dark eyes of hers had tightened with a trace of fear.

He didn't make her ask the question. He answered quietly instead. "I'm coming. I gave you my word."

She hesitated openly, eyes flickering to the rest of his pack. "Yes, but we're really careless about things like that. You don't actually have to—"

"I'm not," he interrupted.

"...what?"

"Careless about things like that." He gazed down at her with a tender smile. "I told you I'm coming. I'm seeing this through." His eyes flicked up sharply. "No matter where it leads."

Ellanden nodded silently, then watched as they walked away.

"Evianna was right," he murmured, "about rushing the prophecy. The realm wasn't ready yet, even Kaleb wasn't ready. It wasn't until the festival that he considered going after the stone."

The princess glanced up in surprise. She hadn't made that connection.

"We weren't ready yet, either," he continued thoughtfully, watching as a door opened at the top of the stairs. "It's like the fates found a way to...to put us on ice, until it was our time."

She followed his gaze as a lovely young woman stepped onto the terrace.

A lot of things weren't ready.

The fae was transfixed, staring the way he'd done in the forest. A hellhound was growling in front of him but his eyes were only for Freya, like he was seeing her for the first time.

Evie fought back a smile, giving him a playful shove. "Well...it's our time now."

He blinked quickly, forcing his gaze away. "It certainly is. And I hope you took this as a lesson in patience, Everly."

"Shut up." She shoved him again with a laugh. "You jumped out that window same as me."

The smile froze on Ellanden's face as his eyes drifted once more over her shoulder. A little tremble shook through him. Then he squared his shoulders with a deep breath.

"Been doing it ever since..."

Before she could ask what he meant, the fae left the others behind—sweeping across the courtyard, cutting smoothly the bustling crowd, coming to a sudden stop in front of the witch...

...and sweeping back her hair with a passionate kiss.

YES!

Evie clapped her hands over her mouth and stared with all the others. Even Seth and Cosette had stopped in astonishment halfway up the stairs, looking like they couldn't believe their eyes.

Freya was perfectly frozen, caught in a moment of shock.

Then suddenly—

"No!" she shrieked, shoving him back. "You don't get to just *do* that anymore!"

"Freya—"

"Don't *Freya*, me!"

"I wasn't trying to—"

"No—shut up and listen! This is *your* fault, Ellanden! Do you understand?" She closed the space between them, jamming a finger into his chest. "This whole thing is *your* fault!"

"...yes."

"Don't argue with me!" she cried. "I was just a kid, all right? I was a kid who fell hopelessly in love with a fairytale prince who saved her from a life of slavery. Of *course* I couldn't get over it! Of *course* I had your bloody picture on my wall! But none of that was supposed to matter, because the second Cosette and I found you I was going to realize I was wrong!"

"Sweetheart, I'm agreeing with you—"

She smacked him again for silence. "I was going to figure out there were no such things as fairytales. You would become something human. You would have these obvious flaws. And that would wipe the slate clean. I could forget about how I felt and start over. What were the odds I'd fall in love with you twice?"

Her eyes filled with tears, even as she struck him again.

"But then I walked out of the forest and saw you standing there...and you were everything I'd imagined you to be! You were perfect, and I loved you, and...and I can't stop bloody loving you!"

Ellanden pulled in a quick breath, like something had shifted deep inside.

"Freya—"

She slapped down his outstretched hand. "This is YOUR FAULT, Ellanden!"

He nodded slowly.

"Don't just stand there, you idiot! *Say something*!"

A sudden silence fell over the courtyard as her voice echoed off the stones. By now, the entire pack was watching—they weren't even pretending otherwise. The rest of the friends were frozen in breathless anticipation, waiting to see what would happen next.

Ellanden took a step closer, ignoring her angry fists.

"I love you, Freya."

The witch opened her mouth, but he pressed a soft finger to her lips. Those fists were gripping him now. His eyes sparkled with a breathtaking smile.

"It occurs to me…I may have forgotten to say it before."

The rest of the world seemed to fall away as the two of them came together—eyes closed in long-awaited contentment, fingers winding through each other's hair.

But the witch stopped just an inch away, looking up into his eyes.

"It's been ten years since you kissed anyone."

He bit his lip with a mischievous smile. "There was that nymph—"

"Stop talking."

There was no real describing the kiss that followed. It was a kiss from two people who had been waiting to kiss for a very long time. Of course, it didn't last very long.

"Hey there!"

Ellanden startled as a sudden hand clapped him on the shoulder, pulling back to find himself staring into Seth's smiling face. Cosette wasn't far behind him, grinning ear to ear.

"Oh, I'm sorry!" The shifter stared between them in mock horror, using his finger to trace the line. "Were you two having a moment? And I interrupted? That's just *terrible*—"

"Is this what you want?" Ellanden interrupted shortly. Much to everyone's surprise, his eyes were on Cosette. "This is the man you want? Even when you know how it ends?"

The smile froze on Seth's face as Cosette nodded slowly.

"This is what I want. This is *who* I want."

Ellanden stared at her a long moment, then abruptly nodded. "Then I'll support you."

The lovely fae beamed with a smile the likes of which the others had never seen. As if actual lights had been placed behind her eyes, painting her in a soft glow of pure, incandescent happiness.

The shifter was wary and unsure, still fixed upon Ellanden.

"Just like that?"

"Just like that."

"It's that simple?"

"It's that simple."

Slowly, *very* slowly, the shifter began to smile. It was a smile that broadened as he convinced himself the prince wasn't about to pull a blade.

"So you'll support it," he repeated, something that carried much more weight seeing as he was about to fly off and meet her parents. "That's something."

Ellanden nodded curtly as the others began talking. "It's quite something indeed."

The shifter smiled again, pressing his luck. "And if I was immortal...you would *approve* of me and Cosette?"

Evie snorted with laughter, and Asher looked away to hide a grin.

"No," the fae answered decisively, before adding, "but I wouldn't openly object."

"Because I don't deserve her?"

"Because you don't come *close* to deserving her."

Seth smiled again, shaking his head. "Then why did you save me that day by the forest?"

The fae cursed in his native language. "Because you make her divinely happy—you moron!"

It was as close to friendship as the two had ever come.

The fae strode away a moment later, Freya gripping his hand. Seth and Cosette were quick to follow, vanishing up the opposite stairwell to gather the remains of their things. Evie and Asher were left standing alone in the courtyard, staring after them with matching smiles.

"I think we witnessed some major progress today in terms of Ellanden's personality," Asher remarked casually. "We may have to find him a gold star."

The princess snorted with laughter. "Don't bother. Give him one and he'll just want two." She paused, considering. "Then he'll complain they're too small."

The vampire chuckled, then laced his fingers with hers. "You know...when I said that we should tell our parents everything..." He hesitated ever so slightly, a rush of nerves sweeping over his face. "...maybe we should amend that a little."

She looked up with a coy grin. "Is someone getting cold feet?"

He didn't quite deny it. "Someone spent his entire childhood watching your father tear grown men to pieces." An actual shudder ran through his hand. "And then there's your mother..."

Evie grinned again, squeezing him tighter. "I think we can probably wait a little on that one. You know, give them time to adjust."

"For their own good," he added quickly.

"Yeah—for their own good."

They paused a moment, staring at the eastern horizon.

Whatever magic the fae called down from the heavens wasn't leaving anytime soon. Rays of unfiltered sunlight glinted off the lofty towers, not a cloud in the sky.

"I can't believe we're going to see them," she whispered, holding tighter to his hand. "After all this time...I can't believe it's finally here."

He nodded silently, a war of emotions dancing in his eyes.

"We're going to fix this," she continued, stepping into his line of sight. "I know it seemed hopeless, Ash...but we're going to set things right."

His eyes rested on her a moment, then warmed with a smile. "I know we are."

It just might take a little time.

Doors were opening and closing above them. Seth was kissing his mother goodbye as the rest of them said farewell to the pack.

Evie watched a bit nervously, having never carried anyone before let alone flown a great distance. She knew she could—her mother had been able to. Now there was a lot of build-up now to this single moment. She suddenly hoped she'd be able to transform again.

"You're hoping for another hellhound, aren't you?" Asher asked with a sudden grin.

She scoffed dismissively. "...don't be ridiculous."

Though it might help.

At the last possible moment, a beautiful woman swept down the stairs—her hands were empty and her eyes were shining with an impossible smile. If there was one person even more excited about the prospect of finding their parents, it was Adelaide Grey.

"It's time, my darling." She came to a stop in front of them as the rest of the friends gathered behind. "Are you ready?"

Evie glanced once more around the fortress before taking a deep breath.

"We're about to find out..."

The courtyard was emptied. A hundred pairs of eager eyes watched from the slatted windows as the princess stood by herself in the middle of the deserted stones. Her eyes were closed and her arms drifted out beside her. Though she'd never know, the pack's children would speak of the moment forever after—the moment the dragon sprang to life.

There was burst of fire—she felt bad about that later. But it fired into the air, leaving no damage left behind. Her friends stared after it, looking highly uncertain. Then with a sudden burst of determination they strode forward—climbing onto her outstretched wing.

Asher was the last one in line. Instead of sitting on her back with the others he climbed to the base of her neck—leaning down with a soft kiss before stretching forward to catch her eye.

"You said it yourself, love...it's our time."

She pulled in a breath then turned toward the horizon, the light of adventure shining in her eyes. Those magnificent wings lifted and they shot into the sky.

Ready to see what the next chapter had in store...

THE END

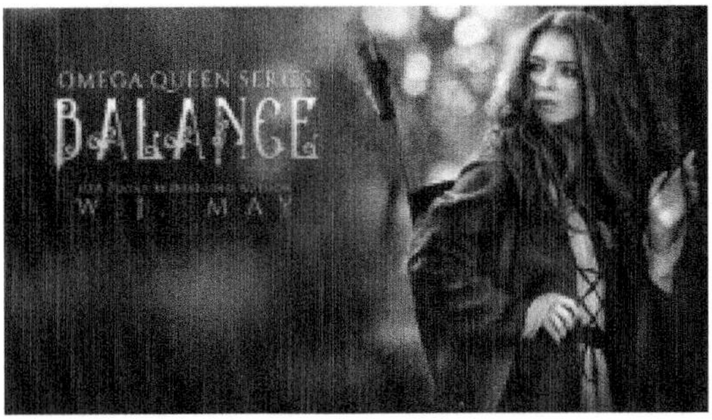
OMEGA QUEEN SERIES
BALANCE
W J MAY

Book #9 BALANCE

WHO SAYS YOU CAN'T go home again?

When a crimson dragon rises from the ancient fortress, Evie and her friends think their luck is finally turning. Their enemy is strong, but not invincible. He is raising an army of darkness, but they have powerful allies to come to their aid. They are returning to their parents. Their parents will know what to do.

If only things were so simple.

A realm divided cannot stand, and it will take more than taking up the crown again to restore the five kingdoms. Sacrifices must be made, an impossible choice that shakes the friends to their very core.

Are they willing to do what is required? Can they set aside personal happiness for the greater good?

No matter what they're forced to give...will it ever be enough?

The Queen's Alpha Series

Eternal
Everlasting
Unceasing
Evermore
Forever
Boundless
Prophecy
Protected
Foretelling
Revelation
Betrayal
Resolved

The Omega Queen Series

Discipline
Bravery
Courage
Conquer
Strength
Validation
Approval
Blessing
Balance
Grievance
Enchanted
Gratified

Find W.J. May

Website:
http://www.wjmaybooks.com
Facebook:
https://www.facebook.com/pages/Author-WJ-May-FAN-PAGE/141170442608149
Newsletter:
SIGN UP FOR W.J. May's Newsletter to find out about new releases, updates, cover reveals and even freebies!
http://eepurl.com/97aYf

More books by W.J. May

The Chronicles of Kerrigan
BOOK I - *Rae of Hope* **is FREE!**
  Book Trailer:
  http://www.youtube.com/watch?v=gILAwXxx8MU
  Book II - *Dark Nebula*
  Book Trailer:
  http://www.youtube.com/watch?v=Ca24STi_bFM
  Book III - *House of Cards*
  Book IV - *Royal Tea*
  Book V - *Under Fire*
  Book VI - *End in Sight*
  Book VII – *Hidden Darkness*
  Book VIII – *Twisted Together*
  Book IX – *Mark of Fate*
  Book X – *Strength & Power*
  Book XI – *Last One Standing*
  BOOK XII – *Rae of Light*

PREQUEL –
Christmas Before the Magic
Question the Darkness
Into the Darkness
Fight the Darkness
Alone the Darkness
Lost the Darkness

SEQUEL –
    Matter of Time
    Time Piece
    Second Chance
    Glitch in Time
    Our Time
    Precious Time

BLESSING

Hidden Secrets Saga:
Download Seventh Mark part 1 For FREE
Book Trailer:
http://www.youtube.com/watch?v=Y-_vVYC1gvo

Like most teenagers, Rouge is trying to figure out who she is and what she wants to be. With little knowledge about her past, she has questions but has never tried to find the answers. Everything changes when she befriends a strangely intoxicating family. Siblings Grace and Michael, appear to have secrets which seem connected to Rouge. Her hunch is confirmed when a horrible incident occurs at an outdoor party. Rouge may be the only one who can find the answer.

An ancient journal, a Sioghra necklace and a special mark force life-altering decisions for a girl who grew up unprepared to fight for her life or others.

All secrets have a cost and Rouge's determination to find the truth can only lead to trouble...or something even more sinister.

RADIUM HALOS - THE SENSELESS SERIES
Book 1 is FREE

Everyone needs to be a hero at one point in their life.

The small town of Elliot Lake will never be the same again.

Caught in a sudden thunderstorm, Zoe, a high school senior from Elliot Lake, and five of her friends take shelter in an abandoned uranium mine. Over the next few days, Zoe's hearing sharpens drastically, beyond what any normal human being can detect. She tells her friends, only to learn that four others have an increased sense as well. Only Kieran, the new boy from Scotland, isn't affected.

Fashioning themselves into superheroes, the group tries to stop the strange occurrences happening in their little town. Muggings, break-ins, disappearances, and murder begin to hit too close to home. It leads the team to think someone knows about their secret - someone who wants them all dead.

An incredulous group of heroes. A traitor in the midst. Some dreams are written in blood.

Courage Runs Red
The Blood Red Series
Book 1 is FREE

WHAT IF COURAGE WAS your only option?

When Kallie lands a college interview with the city's new hot-shot police officer, she has no idea everything in her life is about to change. The detective is young, handsome and seems to have an unnatural ability to stop the increasing local crime rate. Detective Liam's particular interest in Kallie sends her heart and head stumbling over each other.

When a raging blood feud between vampires spills into her home, Kallie gets caught in the middle. Torn between love and family loyalty she must find the courage to fight what she fears the most and possibly risk everything, even if it means dying for those she loves.

Daughter of Darkness - Victoria
Only Death Could Stop Her Now
The Daughters of Darkness is a series of female heroines who may or may not know each other, but all have the same father, Vlad Montour. Victoria is a Hunter Vampire

HUNTRESS SERIES
USA TODAY BESTSELLING AUTHOR
W.J. MAY
LOOK BACK
MASTER
PERMISSION

PROPHECY SERIES
USA TODAY BESTSELLING AUTHOR
• W.J. MAY •

The Chronicles of
KERRIGAN
W.J. May
RAE OF HOPE
DARK NEBULA
HOUSE OF CARDS
ROYAL TEA
UNDER FIRE
END IN SIGHT
KERRIGAN

THE HIDDEN
SECRETS SAGA
W.J. MAY
THE HIDDEN
SECRETS SAGA

Don't miss out!

Visit the website below and you can sign up to receive emails whenever W.J. May publishes a new book. There's no charge and no obligation.

https://books2read.com/r/B-A-SSF-YAVJB

BOOKS 2 READ

Connecting independent readers to independent writers.

Did you love *Blessing*? Then you should read *The Price For Peace*[1] by W.J. May!

How do you keep fighting when you've already been claimed?

When sixteen-year-old Elise is ripped from her home and taken to the royal palace as a permanent 'guest', she thinks her life is over.

Little does she know it has only just begun...

After befriending a group of other captives, including the headstrong Will, Elise finds herself swept away to a world she never knew existed—polished, sculpted, and refined until she can hardly recognize her own reflection. She should be happy to have escaped the poverty of her former life. But she knows a dark truth.

The palace is a dream on the surface, but a nightmare underneath.

---

1. https://books2read.com/u/38EZXr

2. https://books2read.com/u/38EZXr

With a dwindling population, the royals have imprisoned the teenagers to marry and breed. Only seven days remain of freedom before they will be selected by a courtier and forever claimed.

Danger lurks around every corner. The only chance of escape is death.

But when the day of the claiming finally arrives...the world will never be the same.

Royal Factions
The Price for Peace – Book 1
The Cost for Surviving – Book 2
The Punishment for Deception – Book 3
Faking Perfection – Book 4
The Most Cherished – Book 5
The Strength to Endure – Book 6
Read more at www.wjmaybooks.com.

Also by W.J. May

Bit-Lit Series
Lost Vampire
Cost of Blood
Price of Death

Blood Red Series
Courage Runs Red
The Night Watch
Marked by Courage
Forever Night
The Other Side of Fear
Blood Red Box Set Books #1-5

Daughters of Darkness: Victoria's Journey
Victoria
Huntress
Coveted (A Vampire & Paranormal Romance)
Twisted
Daughter of Darkness - Victoria - Box Set

Great Temptation Series
The Devil's Footsteps
Heaven's Command
Mortals Surrender

Hidden Secrets Saga
Seventh Mark - Part 1
Seventh Mark - Part 2
Marked By Destiny
Compelled
Fate's Intervention
Chosen Three
The Hidden Secrets Saga: The Complete Series

Kerrigan Chronicles
Stopping Time
A Passage of Time
Ticking Clock
Secrets in Time
Time in the City
Ultimate Future
Guilt Of My Past

Mending Magic Series
Lost Souls
Illusion of Power

Challenging the Dark
Castle of Power
Limits of Magic
Protectors of Light

Omega Queen Series
Discipline
Bravery
Courage
Conquer
Strength
Validation
Approval
Blessing

Paranormal Huntress Series
Never Look Back
Coven Master
Alpha's Permission
Blood Bonding
Oracle of Nightmares
Shadows in the Night
Paranormal Huntress BOX SET

Prophecy Series
Only the Beginning
White Winter
Secrets of Destiny

Revamped Series
Hidden
Banished
Converted

Royal Factions
The Price For Peace
The Cost for Surviving
The Punishment For Deception
Faking Perfection
The Most Cherished
The Strength to Endure

The Chronicles of Kerrigan
Rae of Hope
Dark Nebula
House of Cards
Royal Tea
Under Fire
End in Sight
Hidden Darkness
Twisted Together
Mark of Fate
Strength & Power
Last One Standing
Rae of Light
The Chronicles of Kerrigan Box Set Books # 1 - 6

The Chronicles of Kerrigan: Gabriel
Living in the Past
Present For Today
Staring at the Future

The Chronicles of Kerrigan Prequel
Christmas Before the Magic
Question the Darkness
Into the Darkness
Fight the Darkness
Alone in the Darkness
Lost in Darkness
The Chronicles of Kerrigan Prequel Series Books #1-3

The Chronicles of Kerrigan Sequel
A Matter of Time
Time Piece
Second Chance
Glitch in Time
Our Time
Precious Time

The Hidden Secrets Saga
Seventh Mark (part 1 & 2)

The Kerrigan Kids
School of Potential
Myths & Magic
Kith & Kin
Playing With Power
Line of Ancestry
Descent of Hope
Illusion of Shadows
Frozen by the Future

The Queen's Alpha Series
Eternal
Everlasting
Unceasing
Evermore
Forever
Boundless
Prophecy
Protected
Foretelling
Revelation
Betrayal
Resolved
The Queen's Alpha Box Set

The Senseless Series
Radium Halos - Part 1
Radium Halos - Part 2

Nonsense
Perception
The Senseless - Box Set Books #1-4

Standalone
Shadow of Doubt (Part 1 & 2)
Five Shades of Fantasy
Zwarte Nevel
Shadow of Doubt - Part 1
Shadow of Doubt - Part 2
Four and a Half Shades of Fantasy
Dream Fighter
What Creeps in the Night
Forest of the Forbidden
Arcane Forest: A Fantasy Anthology
The First Fantasy Box Set

Watch for more at www.wjmaybooks.com.

About the Author

About W.J. May

Welcome to USA TODAY BESTSELLING author W.J. May's Page! SIGN UP for W.J. May's Newsletter to find out about new releases, updates, cover reveals and even freebies! http://eepurl.com/97aYf

Website: http://www.wjmaybooks.com

Facebook: http://www.facebook.com/pages/Author-WJ-May-FAN-PAGE/141170442608149?ref=hl *Please feel free to connect with me and share your comments. I love connecting with my readers.*

W.J. May grew up in the fruit belt of Ontario. Crazy-happy childhood, she always has had a vivid imagination and loads of energy. After her father passed away in 2008, from a six-year battle with cancer (which she still believes he won the fight against), she began to write again. A passion she'd loved for years, but realized life was too short to keep putting it off. She is a writer of Young Adult, Fantasy Fiction and where ever else her little muses take her.

Read more at www.wjmaybooks.com.